LOVE INSPIRED
INSPIRATIONAL ROMANCE

Uplifting stories of faith, forgiveness and hope.

Fall in love with stories where faith helps guide you through life's challenges, and discover the promise of a new beginning.

AVAILABLE THIS MONTH

ISBN-13: 978-1-335-58524-0

EAN

LOVE INSPIRED
INSPIRATIONAL ROMANCE

An Amish Proposal for Christmas

VANNETTA CHAPMAN
USA TODAY BESTSELLING AUTHOR

Her deepest Christmas wish
will bring more than she
imagined...

"I didn't mean to make you sad..."

The tune for "O Come, All Ye Faithful" popped into Becca's head. She didn't realize she was humming it until Gideon gave her a look, and then they both laughed at the same time.

"Maybe you inherited your love for Christmas from your *mamm*."

Becca sat up straighter. "You could be right. I remember stringing popcorn and berries and wrapping it around the porch railing with her. And baking cookies. And sitting next to her as *Dat* read the Christmas story."

He smiled and said, "One mystery explained— the origin of Becca's Christmas fascination." He pulled up a handful of weeds, tossed them in the air and smiled like he'd done something noteworthy.

She caught herself staring at his hands, remembering what they'd felt like holding hers. She shook her head, attempting to clear it, then gave up and pressed her palms against her cheeks.

"Am I giving you a headache?"

"You are."

"Should I go?" His voice had dropped an octave. "I will, if you want me to. It's just that…"

"What?"

"I've missed you, Becca…"

Vannetta Chapman has published over
one hundred articles in Christian family magazines
and received over two dozen awards from
Romance Writers of America chapter groups.
She discovered her love for the Amish while
researching her grandfather's birthplace of Albion,
Pennsylvania. Her first novel, *A Simple Amish
Christmas*, quickly became a bestseller. Chapman
lives in Texas Hill Country with her husband.

Books by Vannetta Chapman

Love Inspired

Indiana Amish Market

An Amish Proposal for Christmas

Indiana Amish Brides

A Widow's Hope
Amish Christmas Memories
A Perfect Amish Match
The Amish Christmas Matchmaker
An Unlikely Amish Match
The Amish Christmas Secret
An Amish Winter
"Stranded in the Snow"
The Baby Next Door
An Amish Baby for Christmas
The Amish Twins Next Door

Visit the Author Profile page at LoveInspired.com.

An Amish Proposal
for Christmas

Vannetta Chapman

LOVE INSPIRED
INSPIRATIONAL ROMANCE

LOVE INSPIRED®
INSPIRATIONAL ROMANCE

ISBN-13: 978-1-335-58524-0

An Amish Proposal for Christmas

Copyright © 2022 by Vannetta Chapman

For questions and comments about the quality of this book, please contact us at CustomerService@Harlequin.com.

Love Inspired
22 Adelaide St. West, 41st Floor
Toronto, Ontario M5H 4E3, Canada
www.LoveInspired.com

Printed in U.S.A.

There is no fear in love.
—*1 John* 4:18

How do I love thee? Let me count the ways.
I love thee to the depth and breadth and height
My soul can reach.
—Elizabeth Barrett Browning

This book is dedicated to my readers.

Chapter One

Shipshewana, Indiana, May 17

Rebecca Yoder checked her reflection in the ladies' room mirror at the Shipshewana Outdoor Market—the largest outdoor market in the Midwest, if the town's advertisement flyers were to be believed. Large or not, she couldn't wait to be far from this place. Any direction would do, just not here. She straightened her apron, made sure her *kapp* was properly fastened and threw back her shoulders.

She could do this.

Train her replacement. Confirm her position with the mission board. Start living life on her own terms.

She marched down the hall and tapped on the closed door with *General Manager* stenciled on the front. Her *dat* called out, "Come in," so she did. He was sitting with Gideon Fisher, the new hire who was to take her place.

Becca hadn't actually met Gideon, but she'd heard plenty about him. He was the middle child of nine siblings, and his parents were longtime friends of her *dat*. Apparently, they'd asked that Amos find a place for

Gideon at the market. He was born and raised in the small Amish community of Beeville in South Texas.

Texas. To Becca, even a small town in nowhere Texas sounded better than Northern Indiana.

"Rebecca, come in. I want you to meet Gideon."

She smiled in what she hoped was a friendly and confident manner and took the seat next to Gideon. "*Gut* to meet you, Gideon."

"And you, Rebecca." He said her name with a southern drawl that reminded her of a slow-moving river.

"Becca is fine."

He nodded as if that made sense, but he didn't comment.

She knew from what her *dat* had shared that Gideon was a bit shy, but he managed to make eye contact before glancing away.

He looked to be a tall man, though she couldn't really tell since he was seated. He had blond hair and blue eyes.

Why was he so shy?

None of that mattered. The only thing she needed to be concerned with was that he take the job permanently so she could escape this place.

Her *dat* was still looking at her with a Cheshire cat grin, which usually meant he was up to something—and usually that something was matchmaking. Now, which of her four *schweschdern* did he have in mind for Gideon? She almost felt sorry for the man sitting beside her, but she quickly pushed away any such sentiments. If he fell for one of her *schweschdern*, he'd be more likely to stay, keep the job and survive the ninety-day trial period.

As soon as he did that, she was free.

"Gideon is eager to begin today."

"As am I." She turned to toss another smile at Gideon. "I can't wait to show you our *wunderbaar* market."

"It's bigger than I imagined."

"Oh *ya*—biggest in the Midwest." She nearly slapped her forehead. To her ears, she sounded like one of the Shipshe flyers. "We'll have you up to speed in no time."

"It's a lot to learn," Amos cautioned. "Becca has been helping here at the market since she was old enough to count out change."

"All of my life." She tried to make that sound like a good thing.

"Rest assured that I'm putting your training in her competent hands."

Her *dat* had recently turned fifty-six. They teased him often about his beard, which was mostly gray now, and his brown hair, which was still putting up a fight. He was round and usually jolly, though quite serious at work. His wire-rim spectacles gave him a solemn look.

"He might not even need ninety days," she suggested. "I suspect Gideon will be a fast learner."

"Becca, we will not rush this."

"Oh, I wasn't—"

"It's very important that Gideon shadow you for the first thirty days. Gideon, I expect you to take notes and ask questions."

Gideon nodded again, but this time the corners of his mouth were turned down.

Becca barely resisted rolling her eyes. It wasn't as if he'd be expected to perform surgery. It was an outdoor market—didn't take a genius to manage the vendors, oversee the auction, maintain the calendar, schedule deliveries and hold meetings.

"After the initial thirty days, the second month of

your internship is when you'll split the responsibilities with Becca, cycling through each section of the market until you're comfortable with every facet of your job."

Becca would only be working part-time at that point. She could begin preparing for her position with Mennonite Disaster Services. She wondered where her first assignment would be. Perhaps in Oregon, which suffered with wildfires nearly every August. Or maybe there would be flooding in Tennessee. Not that she hoped for such a terrible thing, but she'd always wanted to see the Smoky Mountains.

"Finally, Becca will be available for the final thirty days of your ninety-day trial period, to answer questions or help with emergencies."

The last emergency she remembered was the cotton candy machine breaking down in the snack bar. Becca was pretty sure Gideon could handle things on his own, but she nodded enthusiastically. It was easier—and more expedient—to go along with her father's plan. Disagreeing with him, especially in matters related to the market, was a lesson in frustration.

"Do either of you have any questions?"

"We'll be fine, *Dat*. Try not to worry."

"I'm the general manager. Worrying is part of my job description."

Becca glanced at her watch. "Eight thirty. Gates are open, so I suppose we should get started." She popped out of her chair.

"Wait—here's a schedule." Amos handed her a slip of paper filled from top to bottom with his neat handwriting. Her *dat* was famous for his small slips of paper that invariably contained lists of things she didn't want to do.

She scanned it quickly, then passed it to Gideon. "I'm ready if you are, Gideon."

He was now standing, but held back when she walked to the door. "Thank you, Amos. I appreciate you giving me this opportunity."

"We're happy to have you here. Becca will be able to answer any questions you have. All of my *doschdern* know this market as well as they know their own home." He hesitated as if he wanted to say more, shook his head and then motioned for them to go.

They were out of the office, down the hall and out of the building before Gideon managed to say what was on his mind. "Any idea what that was about?"

"What *what* was about?"

"Your *dat* thinking I need a babysitter."

"He never said that."

Their first stop was the vendor spaces outside the auction building. Gideon turned left. Becca snagged his arm and nodded toward the right.

"He could have simply given me the list."

"He could have, but then you might have ended up in the livestock barn when you're supposed to be in the auction building."

"Honest mistake."

"Look." She stopped in the middle of a walkway teeming with people—Amish, *Englisch*, young and old. The day was achingly beautiful, and it flashed through Becca's mind that she might actually miss this place. Couldn't miss it until you left, though, and leaving would only be possible if she convinced Gideon to stay. "*Dat* is very glad you accepted the position of assistant manager."

"He said that? Because he looked rather skeptical."

"He treats this market like it's his lifework, which I suppose it is."

Gideon glanced around the crowded aisle where they were standing. Studying him more closely, Becca realized he looked as if he'd stepped off the cover of an Amish novel. Perhaps her youngest *schweschder*, Ada, would take a liking to him. Ada had recently turned eighteen and was always on the lookout for a new beau, though her relationships tended to have a two- to three-week shelf life.

"How old are you?"

"Twenty-eight. Why?"

Drats. Ten years might be too big of a gap. She discarded the idea of matching him up with Ada. "My oldest *schweschder*, Sarah, is twenty-eight."

Gideon shrugged as if he couldn't care less. Why wasn't he married? He was good-looking enough; though at the moment, those good looks were marred by an expression of utter dismay.

"Are there always this many people?"

"It's a *gut*-sized crowd today. Summers are busy, our special weekends in the fall are busy, even Christmas is busy."

"Christmas?"

"*Ya*, we have a special Christmas market—not on Christmas Day, of course, but the weekend leading up to it."

"Why are we talking about Christmas?"

Becca smiled in what she hoped was a pleasant way. "Because Christmas is my favorite holiday." She started to add that he hadn't seen anything yet, but she didn't want to scare him off. She also thought it best not to add that, in her opinion, a ninety-day trial period was ridiculously long. Surely, three weeks would be enough. Perhaps once her *dat* saw how well Gideon took to the job, he'd change his mind.

"It's a beautiful May day. Folks like to come out and do their shopping when the weather is *gut*."

"Feels a bit cool to me. It's already in the nineties in Texas."

"Is it now?"

Gideon looked a bit homesick.

She needed to distract him, and she needed to do so before he could catch a bus out of town. "Vendors set up in the auction barn are first on the list. Ready?"

She motioned toward the large red building. Gideon absently ran a thumb under his right suspender before shrugging. "Sure. Let's do this."

The list had her guiding Gideon through every part of the market grounds, ostensibly to give him an overall feel for the place. Becca had started helping at the market when she was eleven, but she'd been visiting the market since she could walk. She remembered coming here with her *mamm*.

That thought brought a familiar ache. Her mother had died when she was only seven years old, and yet Becca still felt the pang of loss when she thought of her. Being Amish, they didn't have many photographs taken, but neither were they forbidden. She knew of three that included her mother, all kept in the family keepsake box in the living room. Her memories of her *mamm* were more vivid than those photographs. Still, she sometimes liked to pull one out and trace her fingers over the image.

Her *mamm* had loved the market as much as her *dat* did. They both considered Shipshewana to be the best place in the world to live.

But Becca wasn't like her *mamm* or anyone else in her family. She'd always been the odd girl out. She'd been reading books about other places since she was old enough to borrow them from the library. It seemed ironic that now she was supposed to convince Gideon that the job she couldn't wait to be rid of was the perfect job for him.

"The market has grown a little busier every year," she admitted as they walked toward the auction building. "Shipshewana has become quite the tourist mecca, and many of those people come to our little spot in northeastern Indiana specifically to visit our market and auction."

"How big is this place?"

"Forty acres, with over seven hundred vendor booths."

Gideon let out a long whistle, causing several of the teenaged Amish girls passing by to glance his way. They smiled, put their heads together and giggled behind their hands.

"I thought Shipshewana was a small town."

"It is. Our population is still under a thousand."

"Many towns in Texas are smaller than that."

Was he going to bring up Texas at every turn of the conversation? Becca darted left to avoid being run over by a baby stroller being pushed by a child barely old enough to see over the top. "That's the population in the town limits, but there are many more than that in the surrounding county."

"Oh."

"And market days bring our numbers up to approximately thirty-five thousand folks."

Gideon stopped at that, looking at her in disbelief.

Oops. Maybe she should have held that news back until he'd become acclimated.

She cocked her head. "Did you read up on the place before you accepted the job?"

"I read the job requirements."

"Ah."

"Not sure I read that number. It's rather…alarming."

She smiled brightly, hoping to ease his concerned expression. She'd been in this guy's presence less than fifteen minutes, and she was already learning that *Worried* might as well be stamped on Gideon Fisher's forehead. He had that in common with her *dat*. But how was he going to be a competent assistant manager if he was overwhelmed by the sheer number of people?

Not her problem.

She was sure her *dat* had it all worked out.

Amos Yoder didn't hire someone without checking their background thoroughly and being completely convinced that the applicant was the correct person for the position. Sure, the job offer had also been a favor for his parents, but that didn't mean Gideon couldn't do it. If her *dat* said that Gideon would make a good assistant manager, then Becca shouldn't doubt for a minute that he would.

Once he learned his way around the market.

And stopped gawking at all the people.

And quit comparing everything to Texas.

Gideon felt like he was riding the tilt-a-whirl at the county fair. He wasn't sure he'd ever actually been surrounded by this many people. Rebecca—correction, *Becca*—was easy enough to follow. She marched through the crowd with such authority that the flood of people practically parted to make way for her.

An Amish woman parting the Red Sea.

He almost smiled at the thought, but there wasn't time. She'd darted right, then left, then entered a door marked Employees Only on the side of the auction building. He rushed to catch up with her. How did she move so fast? She was pretty, energetic and a good six inches shorter, with much smaller feet. Yes, he'd checked her out. He certainly wasn't in a place in his life where he wanted to court someone, but he had a beating heart. What man wouldn't notice her?

Personally, he preferred women who weren't so bossy.

She also seemed rather pushy and dismissive. She'd barely acknowledged his comments about Texas. Obviously, she didn't realize what a unique and wonderful place it was. Probably she'd never even been out of Indiana. Many Amish never left the county they were born in. Talking of Texas would be like describing the moon to her—totally irrelevant.

The next three hours passed in a blur of names and buildings. They toured the auction building and the livestock barn. At least the smell of animals brought him some sense of familiarity, even comfort, but they stayed less than twenty minutes before Becca hurried him out to walk up and down the aisles separating the rows of outdoor booths. Over seven hundred vendors sold everything from sunglasses to comic books to soaps and other handmade items.

He slowed near a booth selling cookies and cupcakes and pies. Becca pulled him away. "Three more aisles, then we'll stop for lunch."

The words were more of a command than a suggestion. She smiled, but he saw the steely resolve in her expression. She wasn't his boss. Was she?

Gideon realized in that moment that he was starving.

How long had they been walking through the market? And how much more was there to see?

Apparently, a lot—they sailed past booths with produce, spices, even rugs. Finally, they reached the end of an aisle that bordered the red parking lot.

"Questions?"

"Lots."

"Great. Let's head to the auction restaurant and debrief."

Debrief? Did she just say *debrief*? Was she even Amish?

His mood improved after he'd eaten a roast beef sandwich with fries and a piece of fresh apple pie, plus slugged back three cups of coffee. Maybe the caffeine would help him keep up with her.

Becca had chosen an egg salad sandwich, side salad and chocolate pie.

"Food's *gut*."

"You definitely won't go hungry here."

"How do you do it?" He popped the last piece of apple pie into his mouth, again drained his cup and sat back.

"Do what?"

"All of it—keep up with such a big place, remember everyone's name, handle everyone's crisis?"

Twice she'd been stopped because of vendor disagreements regarding space. She'd handled those deftly, and both vendors had good-naturedly accepted her solution. But when she'd helped a young Amish teenager change the roll of paper on a mobile cash register, he shook his head in disbelief. Was there anything that Becca Yoder didn't know how to do?

"It's not that hard—plus, I've been doing it since I was…"

"Young. Yeah, your *dat* mentioned that."

"Plus, I'm good." She wiggled her eyebrows.

"Modest, too, apparently." He said it softly, but she didn't let it go.

"Is that what you like, Gideon? Modest girls?"

Instead of looking away, he met her gaze. "You know what they say about pride…going before a fall and all that."

"Actually, the proverb says *Pride goeth before destruction, and a haughty spirit before a fall.*"

"Same difference."

"Is it?" She shrugged and finished the last bite of her pie. "I didn't mean to come across as bold or proud. But I am good at this job."

"Then why are you leaving it?" There. He'd asked the question that had been niggling at the back of his mind since meeting her. There must be something wrong here if she was so anxious to leave. "I assumed you were marrying, but…"

"But what, Gideon?" Now her eyes were laughing. She waited, not letting him off the hook he'd put himself on.

"Well, it's just that you haven't mentioned a beau or any wedding plans or…"

"Maybe I don't like talking about personal stuff."

"Maybe."

She checked her watch, then pulled out her *dat*'s list. "We still have the parking lots to cover, all the entrances and exits, rest areas… And I want to show you the scooter rental and ATM machine."

Gideon groaned.

Becca drummed her fingers against the table. "How big is your parents' farm?"

"One hundred and twenty-two acres."

"Fairly large by Amish standards."

"And yet small by Texas standards."

Just the memory of home lowered his blood pressure. How he wished he were there. Why had he left? He should be checking the crops in the fields, not walking the aisles of a market.

"You worked on the farm?"

"Every day—planting, harvesting, checking fence."

"But, see, that's my point. Our entire facility is only forty acres—a third of what you're used to."

Which didn't make him feel a bit better. Becca popped out of the booth, carried her dishes to a bucket and deposited her trash in the receptacle. Only then did she look back to see if he'd followed.

"Ready?"

"Or not…" But they weren't children playing a game of hide-and-seek. He was a grown man. He was a farmer, and he was totally out of his comfort zone at the Midwest's largest outdoor market.

Why had he let his parents talk him into this?

Why hadn't he argued with them?

Somehow, he'd thought that if he came up here, gave this job his best shot and convinced everyone how ill-suited he was for such a venture, his parents would readily dismiss the idea. He'd thought that he'd be home within the week.

Home.

Nausea filled his stomach as he stepped back outside with Becca. He didn't want to be here. He did not like large crowds of people, and he did not remember a single thing that he was supposed to have learned today.

He closed his eyes and pictured the cottonwood trees

next to their creek. He imagined the grain ripening in the fields.

Becca cleared her throat.

He opened his eyes.

Crowds of people, a line of *Englisch* cars and pretty Becca—impatiently tapping her foot.

Exile. That was what this was.

But he could—he *would* find a way home.

Chapter Two

Rebecca was worried on Tuesday. On Wednesday, she practically hit panic mode. Not only was Gideon shy and quiet, but he also made no effort to be pleasant with the various vendors and supervisors. It was as if he didn't understand that *his* success depended on *their* success.

It was almost as if he wasn't planning on staying.

To make matters worse, her *dat* had invited him to dinner on Friday night.

"Why wouldn't I? He's new to town, and we're the only people he knows so far."

"We haven't exactly bonded."

"Whose fault is that?"

"His, *Dat*. It's his fault."

Becca knew that she had her *dat*'s attention when he lowered his paper, ducked his head and stared over the top of his glasses at her.

"Are you worried that he's the wrong person for the job?"

She started backpedaling quickly. "Of course not. I'm just…tired, is all. It's a lot of work to train someone. I don't know how you've managed all these years." Then she fled to the kitchen to help with dinner.

"Sounds like your escape plan is in jeopardy." Sarah tossed her a sympathetic smile.

Sarah was the oldest, and in Becca's opinion also the prettiest. Where Becca was only five foot four, Sarah was five foot ten. She was thinner, too, and had their father's dark brown hair. More than those things, though, her demeanor was something that Becca wished she had: calm, competent—wise, even. Sarah was completely unaware of just how pretty she was. It only added to her attractiveness.

Which made the fact that she was twenty-eight and single even more puzzling. There'd been the one engagement eight years ago. That had ended quite unexpectedly. Becca had been sixteen at the time and completely involved in her own life—that must have been the year her *dat* suggested she'd be an excellent bread baker and arranged for her to work at the Blue Gate Bakery. That was when Becca had first known she didn't have traditional Amish dreams—at least, not traditional for girls.

"Why did you run off from your engagement to Adam?"

"I didn't *run off*." Sarah began to slice a fresh loaf of bread.

Becca reached around her, snagged a piece and spread butter on it. Tearing off a chunk, she popped it into her mouth and shrugged at her *schweschder*'s denial. "If you say so, but local legend remembers it differently."

"Don't lower yourself to heeding gossip."

"I remember it differently too."

Sarah finished slicing the bread and covered it with a clean dish towel. Turning toward Becca, she rested her backside against the sink and crossed her arms. "We were talking about you."

"Uh-huh."

"Why did you ever agree to *Dat*'s deal?"

She studied the rest of her nabbed piece of bread, then popped it into her mouth. It was deliciously warm and yeasty. Bread was definitely one of her favorite things. She supposed they'd have to do with store-bought on mission trips. "It made sense at the time, and you know how he can be…"

"Persuasive."

"I guess." Becca lowered her voice. "I don't want to be the one to disappoint him. I'd rather leave that to Ada."

Their youngest *schweschder* had just walked into the house, carrying a basket filled with early tomatoes from their garden. "I am not a disappointment." She tossed her *kapp* strings over her shoulders. Ada was the baby of the family, and they all adored her. Teasing her was fun, though—maybe because it never seemed to faze her in any way, which only made them try harder.

Becca picked out three of the tomatoes and washed them off in the sink. "*Dat* mentioned you quit your baby-sitting job today."

"Those kids! They were so unruly. You both can shake your heads at me, but caring for two sets of twins is beyond my ability levels. Better to say that the first week, don't you think?"

Ada went on to describe the antics of the four Schwartz children—the twin boys were six years old and the twin girls were four. Apparently, the boys had managed to lock the cat in the old outhouse, which set the dog to barking. By the time Thomas and Timothy had let the cat out, the dog was having such a fit that it set about chasing the tabby cat, who turned and landed a good swipe on the dog's nose. "The girls were crying. The boys were laughing. The dog climbed under the outhouse and wouldn't come out. And the cat sat on the adjacent fence, licking her paws and looking quite pleased with herself."

Bethany walked in just as Ada was describing the events of the day at the Schwartz household. "You quit over a cat-and-dog fight?" She sat down at the table, pulled her current project out of her knitting bag and began working with lavender yarn. Bethany's hands were always busy—knitting, quilting, even hand-stitching designs on pillowcases. The process of creating seemed to bring her immense satisfaction.

Becca envied that about her *schweschder*. Her main feeling these days was restlessness. If she could just train Gideon… If he'd agree to stay… If she could be somewhere else, perhaps she'd experience something like Bethany's contentment.

"That was after the food fight but before the water fight." Ada laughed along with the rest of them. "I'm telling you… I'd need to drink more coffee than Sarah if I was going to handle those children. Remind me to never have twins."

"I'm not sure you'll have any say in that." Bethany glanced up and wiggled her eyebrows as she turned the small sweater she was working on and began to purl. It must be for one of the expectant moms in their church.

It seemed to Becca as if everyone her age and younger was pregnant or hoping to be. She couldn't understand what their hurry was. Everyone was pairing up. Everyone except the Yoder girls—all five of them were happily single, much to their *dat*'s dismay. He was apparently ready for *grandkinner*.

Eunice hurried into the room and began washing her hands at the sink. Eunice was a unique blend of their father and mother—beautiful brown eyes like *Dat*'s but with gorgeous blond hair like *Mamm* had. She was also short like Becca. She'd apparently been working on the generator again, as there was a smudge of grease on her nose.

Eunice peered out the window over the sink. "Looks like your guy is here, Becca."

"He is most certainly not my guy." Becca hurried to the window, though, and she was quickly joined by Sarah, Bethany and Ada. The five of them stood there, staring out at Gideon. He'd apparently borrowed a horse and buggy. He directed the gelding to the hitching post in front of their house, exited the buggy and looked in surprise at the window.

Becca and her *schweschdern* scattered like birds startled by a cat. Before they carried dinner out, each winked at Becca and offered their first impression.

"He's the right age, for once." Sarah nudged Becca's shoulder. "Remember when *Dat* tried to set me up with Widower Hochstetler? He was twenty years my senior."

"Gideon looks nice," Bethany said with a smile, stuffing her knitting back into her bag.

"Plus, he's cute." Ada giggled as she picked up the chicken casserole.

Eunice dried her hands and then slung her arm around Becca's shoulder. "Another of *Dat*'s matchmaking schemes. You'd think that he's in a hurry to be rid of us."

"He's not matching me to Gideon." Becca felt her exasperation rising. "I'm leaving. I already have a position with MDS. I'm going to be spending Christmas in Tennessee or maybe Florida. I've read that in Florida, people decorate palm trees for the holidays. Can you imagine? I certainly won't be here. They're expecting me to show up in August."

"That's what you keep telling us." Sarah handed her a large bowl of salad. At least she softened the teasing with a smile. "Now let's see if you can convince Gideon to stay, because from what you've told us, he hasn't quite taken to Shipshewana."

That was the understatement of the week, but Becca wasn't willing to throw in the towel yet. Perhaps Gideon would show an interest in one of her *schweschdern.* Stranger things had happened.

Unfortunately, dinner didn't go as well as she might have hoped. The food was delicious—as usual. Sarah was a *wunderbaar* cook. They enjoyed chicken casserole, green beans, a very colorful salad and warm bread. Gideon devoured the food, but he didn't tell any funny stories about Texas, and his only comment on the market was "It's been a long week."

He'd only worked four days. How did that equal a long week?

Having all of her *schweschdern* at the table ensured there weren't too many awkward silences.

Ada rattled on about the Schwartz twins. "*Gut* kids, I'm sure, but my goodness. I feel sorry for their parents, for sure and certain I do. Naomi is needed at her parents' home, what with their recent health issues, and John has his hands full trying to care for both farms. Still, I'm glad I figured out early that nannying is not for me."

Becca's *dat* reached for another piece of bread. "No

worries, Ada. We'll find the right job for you—or maybe you'll marry and then you won't need a job."

Gideon choked on his bite of casserole, Ada colored a pretty pink and Sarah jumped up to fetch dessert.

Eunice described the latest project she was working on in the barn—an overhead fan that ran off a solar panel. "I plan to mount it on the ceiling of the back porch this weekend."

No one seemed to know what to say to that. Gideon stared at her as if she'd spoken French. To be fair, Eunice's projects tended to catch them all by surprise. About half of them actually worked the way they were supposed to, though only a quarter of them were practical enough to be of any use. Becca had certainly seen no need for a battery-powered miniature hand rake that Eunice had designed to scratch their old dog's back. Gizmo had whined and trotted off to the field when she'd tried it on him.

By the time they'd eaten dessert and the dishes were cleared, Becca was exhausted. This was one reason she didn't date. It wore a person out trying to figure out what to say or not say, or do or not do.

Gideon must have been thinking the same thing, because he cleared his throat and stood. "I should go. I promised Nathan I'd have his horse and buggy home early."

Becca's *dat* clapped him on the back. "Thanks for coming. We hope you'll make a habit of eating with us."

There was no one left in the room to argue with that except Becca, and she didn't plan on saying a thing. Her *schweschdern* had all vanished: Eunice had excused herself and headed back to the barn; Sarah was in the kitchen, cleaning up; Bethany had gone upstairs to work on her knitting; and Ada had passed on dessert and taken off with a group of *youngies* that was headed to Howie's for ice cream.

Her *dat* had said something to Gideon that she'd missed, but then he ended with "Becca will see you out."

See him out? They were three feet from the front door. She smiled as if she had nothing better to do and walked out onto the front porch with Gideon. To her surprise, he didn't hop into his buggy and leave. Instead, he stopped to scratch Gizmo behind the ears.

"What kind of dog is this?"

"No one seems to know. We think that he might have a little Labrador, beagle and possibly bulldog? Gizmo is a real mystery."

Gideon sighed heavily, as if another mystery was something he did not need. He walked down the steps, then tilted his head back and stared up at the stars.

"The sky is bigger and brighter in Texas."

Ugh. She wanted to scream. She'd heard enough about Texas in the last four days to literally cross the state off her travel map.

"I know that sounds silly..."

"It sounds impossible."

"Yeah. I know." Instead of being offended, Gideon looked at her, then tugged his hat down low. "It's hard to explain how different the Amish community is there. Our homes aren't nearly as nice as yours."

"How so?"

"Most haven't seen a fresh coat of paint in years. There's simply not time or money for such things. It's hard to make a living out of the land. We rarely pass thirty-two inches of rain a year, and five months of each year, our temps are in the nineties or higher."

"Well, I don't know how much rain we get—"

"Thirty-eight inches. I looked it up. Plus, another thirty-four inches of snow. That's why your farms are so green, why the yield is so high."

"Indiana sounds like a *gut* place to settle down. *Ya?*"

Gideon shook his head, and a light blush crept up his neck. "You'd think that easier would be better, but I'm not so sure. Texas is what I know."

"Maybe you'll like Shipshe better in the winter."

"If I'm still here—"

"We have a town Christmas parade, and the Blue Gate Restaurant goes all out with their extravaganza."

"Extravaganza?"

"There's even a gingerbread house contest. Most everyone decorates their yards, even some of the Amish— though not electrical lights, of course."

"You really do love Christmas."

"What's not to love? There's the baby Jesus, the family meal—plus, finding special presents for those you care about. It's the happiest day of the year."

She followed him over to the buggy and Nathan's old gelding. She walked up to the horse, scratched it between the ears and then leaned her forehead against it. Horses were much simpler than people.

"I can't figure you out."

Her head jerked up. "I didn't realize you were trying."

He shrugged rather sheepishly. "We work together. You're training me to take your place. It's unusual enough to have an Amish woman who is an assistant manager—"

"Many Amish women work."

"If you say so. Obviously, you're *gut* at the job."

"Danki."

"So why are you quitting?" He folded his arms and rested his back against the buggy.

Plainly, he wasn't leaving until he had an answer, and Becca didn't want to stand around outside, staring up at the stars with Gideon Fisher. She had a new edition of the MDS newsletter to read. Plus, he was going to find out eventually. Ada had nearly spilled the beans twice, and it was only by kicking her under the table that Becca had been able to stop her. Why should she even care if Gideon knew her plans? It felt private, though, like something she didn't want to share with this man she barely knew. Perhaps he would settle for a portion of the truth.

"I'm not quitting so much as I'm leaving."

"Leaving…" He considered that a moment. "Where are you going?"

"I'm not sure."

He blew out a heavy sigh. "That doesn't make any sense."

"It does. It's what I want to do." She'd been struggling with how to tell him, but now the words came out in a rush. "I've accepted another position that is…well, it's out of state. I'm not sure where I'll be assigned, and it doesn't really matter, because it will be somewhere different. It won't be here."

Gideon laughed. It was the first time she'd heard the sound from him, and it did a lot to erase the perpetual look of worry on his face.

"What's so funny?"

"You've spent the last four days trying to convince me what a great place Shipshe is—"

"It *is* a great place."

"What a *wunderbaar* job assistant director at the Shipshewana Outdoor Market is."

"It *is* a *wunderbaar* job. You should be grateful that my *dat* offered it to you."

"And yet you can't wait to be rid of it." He straightened and stepped closer to her. "I think there's something you're not telling me."

"No, there's not."

"Something that is sending you scurrying away."

"I'm not scurrying."

"Because if it were as *gut* as you claim, who would want to leave?"

Becca didn't have an answer for that. She'd never had an answer for that, so she stood there silently as he climbed into the buggy, called out to the horse and drove away. But she walked back into the house with his question circling through her mind: *If it were as gut as you claim, who would want to leave?*

Gideon spent Saturday working in Nathan's garden. He'd agreed to do chores around the old man's farm in exchange for a place to stay, and he didn't mind the work. It helped take his mind off *the job* and *the woman*. He always thought of both as if they were bolded and underlined in a novel.

What had he got himself into?

He dreaded the thought of going back to the market on Monday, and only one thing kept him from catching the next bus back to Texas: he simply could not disappoint his parents. Which meant he'd have to make them understand. He stewed over that much of Saturday and even Sunday as he sat on a church bench, hearing very little of the sermon.

The particulars of the service were similar enough to their services back home that it only caused him to feel more homesick. By the time they had sung the last note of the last hymn and he was in line for lunch, he'd worked himself into quite a discontented place. He filled his plate, then looked for Nathan, who was sitting with a group of older couples. Nathan was a widow. Though Gideon had lived with him less than a week, he knew the old guy was still adjusting to life without his wife.

He was walking toward Nathan's table when Becca popped up in front of him. She was holding a cup of iced tea and a plate of food and looked fresh and energetic— the opposite of how he felt.

"Why don't you come eat with us?"

"Us?" He squinted at her, trying to figure out what she meant. He had absolutely no intention of sitting with all her *schweschdern*. He'd never been around that many women at once. He certainly didn't care to repeat the experience. They seemed to have some silent communication that he didn't understand, and he'd been fairly certain that Becca had kicked one *schweschder* under the table. What was that about?

Didn't know.

Didn't want to know.

"No thanks. Tell your *schweschdern* hello for me, though."

"I didn't mean with my family. We tend to each go our own way at church luncheons. I meant over there." She nodded toward a table full of men and women approximately their age.

"Uh, no. I need to sit with Nathan."

Becca peered in the direction he had indicated. "Nathan's doing just fine without you. Come on. At least be polite enough to meet everyone."

It was the last thing he wanted to do, but when she

put it that way, he didn't feel right arguing. Instead, he followed her. Everyone crowded in to make space. They seemed like a jolly enough crowd, but Gideon could not fit one more name in his head. He ate as quickly as possible, responded to their polite questions as briefly as he could and escaped the minute he thought it was polite to do so.

The service was held at Bishop Ezekiel's. The man had a fair-sized farm, and as soon as Gideon walked toward the pasture holding three paint horses, he felt the tension leave his shoulders. He was standing there, arms over the fence rail, trying to puzzle his way out of this situation, when he heard someone clear their throat. Turning, he almost groaned when he saw Becca.

"That happy to see me, huh?"

"Sorry. I was just…taking a moment."

She joined him at the fence. She allowed a whole fifteen seconds of silence before she jumped in. "Want to tell me what's really bothering you?"

"You wouldn't understand."

"How could you possibly know that?"

"Because you can't wait to leave your home, and I just want to get back to mine."

Instead of being offended, she shrugged. "That makes us different, but it doesn't mean we can't understand each other."

"Fine. You want to know what's wrong with me?" He began to tick items off on his fingers. "I don't like crowds. I miss home. I'm not allowed to make my own decisions."

He stared at his fingers, then shook his head and dropped his hands. "I suppose everything else stems from those three."

"Okay. Well, first of all, the word *crowd* is sort of relative."

"What does that mean?"

"Given our crowds at the market—" she put virtual quote marks around the word *crowds*, which only served to irritate him "—and your discomfort around them, I'd think that you would have enjoyed today more."

He looked at her in disbelief, then waved back toward the large group of people spread out under the trees. "This is a crowd, too, Becca. My church back home isn't half this size."

"Is that why you were so rude to my friends?"

"I was not."

"You were, Gideon. You barely spoke, and you left as soon as you'd gulped down your food."

Her remark hurt more than it should have. He'd never been a rude person. He certainly hadn't intended to come across that way. Just one more example of how he was messing up in this community. He did not belong here.

"Point two—you miss home. That's quite obvious by how you talk about Texas constantly."

"I do not."

"Then why am I suddenly an expert on the great state of Texas? I know that during May, the wildflowers— the bluebonnets—are changing to Indian paintbrushes. I'm aware the crops you grow include cotton, grain and soybean. And I also know that you consider your community to be poor versus our community, which you see as immensely wealthy—something *I* don't see at all."

He shook his head in disbelief. He opened his mouth to argue with her, but she wasn't done yet.

"Also, you don't paint your houses often, and you have

less rain than Shipshe, hotter temperatures and almost no snow. Therefore, farming is harder."

"I'm rather surprised you were paying attention."

Becca tapped the side of her head. "I can listen and walk at the same time."

"Everything's better in Texas, in my opinion. You can't see that because you've only lived here."

"Something I'm trying to change."

"I would be embarrassed for you to see my parents' house. Here…your houses look as if they belong in a *Plain & Simple Magazine*."

"Good grief. So we're wealthy because we paint our houses?"

"That's only one example."

"Okay. Well, I understand that you're homesick, but that will pass."

"How would you know that?"

She actually drew back, glanced around and then met his gaze. "I guess I wouldn't, it's just that…well, I can't imagine being homesick. When I leave in August, I'm sure I'll miss my family and friends, but…it's not as if I won't be able to come back and visit."

"Visiting isn't the same."

"Oh, Gideon. You're miserable because you want to be miserable."

"I do not."

"You've been here six days—"

"Seven. I arrived on Monday and met you on Tuesday. That makes today day seven."

She hung her head in exasperation, but then she looked up and stepped closer. "Fine, seven days. You haven't given us a chance. You've already decided you won't like it. We are not a huge group. We are not a wealthy group.

And your third reason? You can't make your own decisions? That's foolishness. Of course you can. You do. We all make our own decisions, even if it's only to go along with the decisions other people make."

"It's more complicated than that."

"Because you make it more complicated."

Gideon's anger was spiraling out of control. He couldn't have stopped his next words if he'd tried, and he did not try. "You are one of the most irritating people I've ever met."

"Excellent. Then do your job, and you'll be rid of me by mid-August."

With that, she turned and marched off.

Leaving Gideon to mull over the fact that he was good and truly stuck in this situation, and he had no idea what to do about it.

Disappoint his parents?

Turn tail and run?

Or stick it out and be miserable?

For some reason, none of those options appealed to him.

But he had to do something because this situation simply was not acceptable. He couldn't let his life be dictated by the whims of others. It was time he stood up for himself.

Chapter Three

Becca woke Monday morning with renewed resolve. She had tossed much of the night, struggling with the problem of Gideon. Quite simply, she had two options. She could agree with him that he was a bad fit for their community and poorly equipped to handle the position of assistant manager. That would mean advertising the job, then going through the interview process and choosing a new applicant, after which the ninety-day training period would begin.

Her *dat* had been quite adamant about the terms of her release—which was how she'd come to think of it. She could join MDS with his blessing, but first she must help him find her replacement. She was fine with that. She was a responsible person, after all. It was simply that she wanted to be responsible somewhere else.

If she went the route of looking for someone to replace Gideon, it would almost certainly mean that she'd miss the fall job assignments with MDS. Advertising would take several weeks; interviewing, several more. Even if they found someone quickly, training couldn't start before mid-June, and ninety days from that would be mid-September. The MDS teams were in place by mid-September. She'd be stuck here through the long Indiana winter. Best case? She'd be able to join a service group in the spring. Becca supposed she could live with that, but it wasn't what she wanted. She already felt as if she should have left a year ago. It had taken her a while to work through her emotions, then more months to find the courage to share those emotions with her family.

Option one would work, but she hoped it wouldn't come to that.

Option two was that she needed to address Gideon's concerns. If he felt they were too large a group, she needed to introduce him to small groups. She didn't know what to do about him missing home so much. She'd never been homesick because she'd never been away from home. Perhaps she could simply be more sympathetic rather than telling him he was a fool.

But how could she address his feeling that he wasn't making any of his own decisions? She did understand that well enough. For a long time, she had felt that her *dat* and her older *schweschder* had made all her decisions. It was only when she'd learned to voice her preference that she'd gained some independence. Perhaps she could give Gideon more of a voice in his training. That might alleviate some of his frustration.

She checked her reflection in the mirror, straightened her *kapp* a bit to the left and then headed to the kitchen.

Sarah teased her for humming Christmas songs while she helped make breakfast. "That particular day is still seven months away."

"Uh-huh, well, I happen to think we could use a little Christmas cheer this morning, and Christmas songs are just the thing to brighten your perspective."

"Someone woke up on the sunny side of the buggy. It's *gut* to see you happy."

"What's not to be happy about?" Becca tossed her *kapp* strings over her shoulder. "With the right attitude and a plan...we should be able to accomplish anything. Isn't that right?"

"Maybe. My goal for the day is to weed the garden and finish laundry—neither of which require a large amount of planning."

Eunice came in from the barn. How early had she gone out there? And how had she managed to get grease on her face before breakfast?

Bethany was sitting at the table, working on a hand-stitched pillowcase. Becca stood behind her, studying the pattern of wildflowers, which of course reminded her of Gideon. Ugh. She needed to get him out of her head!

"You don't like it?"

"Actually, I do. It's beautiful."

"Then why the groan?"

"I groaned?"

"You did."

"Worried about something at work."

"Or someone..." Sarah offered.

Bethany smiled, but kept stitching. If her hands were busy, she was happy. She'd always been the most contented of the entire family.

Ada popped in, hair uncombed and apron askew. She covered her mouth with her hand, but everyone heard the yawn.

"Late night, *schweschder*?"

"*Ya*. And I never was one to believe that the early duck got the worms."

"I think it's the early *bird* gets the worm." Becca

smiled at her youngest *schweschder*. Ada managed to mangle every proverb or colloquial saying. They'd taken to calling them Ada-isms.

"Whatever. I'm not keen to be a bird or a duck. I'd rather sleep in! The singing went until midnight." She reached for the mug Sarah handed her. *"Danki."*

"Say, I don't suppose you'd be interested in taking Gideon to one of those singings?"

"Gideon? Gideon Fisher that visited here Friday night?" She peered over her coffee mug. "I don't think he said more than a dozen words—plus, isn't he too old for my group?"

Sarah laughed and Becca couldn't help joining her. *"Ya.* We're old, for sure and certain. I forgot."

"I thought I was the old person in this house." Her *dat* had already been out seeing to the animals. He stood in the mudroom, stomping his boots against the mat and placing his hat on the peg near the door. He might be the manager of the Midwest's largest outdoor market, but he was also a farmer; most Amish men were.

They ate quietly, the sound of birdsong filling the air. Becca loved sitting with her family in the morning, before any crisis had arisen, before she remembered that she didn't want to be here. Which she supposed meant that part of her did want to be here. Home had its advantages. Good grief. She was starting to *think* like Gideon.

Her *dat* handed her a half sheet of paper filled with his precise handwriting. "Thought you might cover those items with Gideon this week."

"You know, *Dat*, Gideon's feeling rather uncertain about this whole thing."

"What whole thing? What do you mean, uncertain?"

It occurred to her that what Gideon had shared with

her might have been told in confidence. So instead of answering either of those questions, she pushed forward with her plan. "I thought that I might ask him what he'd like to learn today. Let him sort of set the pace and direction of his training."

Her *dat* looked at her as if she was wearing suspenders over her dress.

She hurried to assure him. "We'll still cover everything on your list but maybe let him pick the order."

"Well." He wiped his mouth with his napkin, stood and kissed each of his *doschdern* on top of the head. When he came to Becca, he said, "I trust you to see to his training, but he'll need to be acquainted with every aspect of the market."

"*Ya*, of course."

He planted a kiss on top of her head, making her feel four years old again—and for some reason, causing tears to sting her eyes. Why was she so emotional today? Perhaps she was catching a cold.

"Buggy leaves in twenty minutes," he said as he walked out of the kitchen.

Becca deposited her dishes in the sink.

Ada finally looked and sounded awake. "I can't believe *Dat*'s insisting I look for another job today."

"You didn't exactly have the last one long enough to earn vacation time," Sarah pointed out.

"I wish I was still in school. Those were the *gut* old days, for sure."

All five girls laughed at that, as Ada hadn't been the school's most devoted student. Becca grabbed her purse and checked her reflection in the mirror. It wouldn't do to show up at work looking less than her best. She had realized while tossing and turning that—for better or worse, fair or not—Gideon had a poor opinion of their community.

If she wanted to be free by August, she was going to need to change that.

Gideon squinted his eyes, regarding her suspiciously. "What's the catch?"

"No catch. I was actually listening to what you said yesterday."

He shifted in his chair uncomfortably. They were sitting in Becca's office, which was about the size of a mudroom. Her *dat* had somehow managed to cram in a desk, two chairs and a filing cabinet. There was a window, though it was a small one. He could see the patch of blue sky outside, which reminded him that he'd rather be working in the fields.

Becca cleared her throat, and he turned his attention back to the map of the market she'd handed him.

"You want me to pick what I want to learn."

"Didn't you say that you wanted to make more of your own decisions?"

He dropped the map on her desk. "I was referring to being here at all."

"*Ya.* I picked up on that. The only trouble is that I can't really change where you are—though you can."

He felt his frown turn into a more pronounced scowl. Little Becca Yoder freely dispensed her own kind of wisdom, which she had gained by the ripe old age of…what?

"How old are you? Twenty-two?"

"Twenty-four, and what does that have to do with anything?"

Instead of explaining what he'd been thinking, he shrugged. Twenty-four! He'd thought he knew it all at that age, but he soon learned that life was more complicated than he could have imagined. The last four years had been a real awakening. First, his parents had tried to set him up on dates; then they'd insisted he apprentice with their bishop, who made buggies. How many buggies were needed in a community of a dozen families? Finally, they'd contacted Becca's *dat* and pressured Gideon to apply for the position. It hadn't actually been an ultimatum, but it had felt like one. It was plain that because he was unmarried and not even dating, they didn't know what to do with him.

And he had gone along with their plans because he'd seen what it meant to them. He sighed and leaned forward to study the offending map.

"Explain it to me again."

"Look, it's not that difficult. *Dat* handed me a list this morning…"

Gideon groaned.

He was surprised when that caused her to laugh.

"You have no idea how much I understand that response. Anyway…you expressed that you'd like to make your own decisions. How about this week, we let your interests drive what you learn first? You've had a brief introduction to the market grounds. Look at the map, and tell me what you'd like to focus on today."

He ran a finger from the Backyard Barnyard to the livestock barn.

"I thought we had three weeks left of me shadowing you."

"That doesn't mean we have to be together all day, every day. It simply means you're not on your own yet. Any questions you have, find me and ask. Of course, that's true for the next ninety days, but the point is that no one expects you to know what to do yet."

"I get it. Okay. Farmers tend to divide work on their land into sections. How about I take this northwest quadrant, and you make some suggestions as to what I need to do there?"

"Excellent."

They spent the next thirty minutes going over delivery schedules and quality checks that needed to be done. He left with a list scribbled on a sheet of paper, but it was his own list in his own handwriting. That went a long way toward brightening his outlook.

Except he was completely overwhelmed before the morning had passed. The barnyard was in absolute pandemonium. Several of the goats were loose, and he managed to corral them back into their pens but only after covering his pants in dirt and hay. Apparently, the young man working there was new to the job and had no idea what he was supposed to be doing. Who was training him? Was that Gideon's job?

In addition, the wrong feed had been delivered to the barnyard. Someone had left twelve sacks of bunny food and nothing for the goats, pony, sheep or llama. Not to mention the llama had spit at him. He knew enough about llamas to understand that an unhappy llama was a difficult one. He'd need to speak to the boy about handling the tan-colored animal. It certainly didn't need to be in a petting zoo until it was more settled.

First things first, though. He needed to resolve the missing-feed situation. He had to hurry back to the office to find out what he should do about that. By the time he got there, Becca was gone. He found her on the opposite end of the market in the blue parking lot, checking on a new horse-and-buggy area that was being redone for Amish vendors as well as visitors.

Just seeing her there irritated him to such a degree that even he realized it was irrational. She looked completely at home among the *Englisch* and Amish employees. In fact, they listened to her as if they respected her—and maybe they did. They even laughed at her joke, which he'd thought was quite silly.

"Why couldn't the pony sing in the choir?" She paused for three beats—not too long but not too short. "Because he was a little hoarse."

All the employees laughed except Gideon, who stood at the back, trying to catch her attention. She reminded everyone of their goal for the day; then, as the group broke up, she hurried back to where Gideon was waiting.

"What's wrong?"

"Everything. Some of the goats escaped, the llama is very unsettled and your barnyard manager has no idea what he's doing. More importantly, the wrong feed was delivered. I ran back to the office only to find you were here at the other end of the market."

"I'm rarely in my office. There isn't much time for that."

"Obviously. So how am I supposed to ask you questions?"

She studied him a moment, then smiled. "I have an idea."

Ten minutes later, they were standing in a supply closet, and she was attempting to reach a box on the top shelf.

"I got it." He retrieved it, resisting the urge to ask how this was going to help him with a lost feed delivery.

The first box she opened was filled with Christmas

things. She pulled out a red-and-green-striped hat with white trim, placed it on top of her *kapp* and smiled.

"Please don't say ho-ho-ho."

She actually looked kind of cute in the hat, but he wasn't about to encourage her Christmas obsession. She grabbed another box, balanced it on a lower shelf, opened it and pulled out two walkie-talkies. "I should have thought of this sooner."

Gideon hadn't held a walkie-talkie since he was a *youngie*. For a while, he and his *bruders* had a pair that they'd carried around. The problem had been charging them. After a few weeks, they'd ended up in the barn, on a shelf, gathering dust.

Becca blew off some dust, then turned her device on and smiled when the light turned green. "They held their charge. Cool."

"Cool?"

She tilted her head at him. "You're pretty uptight."

"Are these approved by your bishop?" He felt old and cranky asking such a thing, but the question popped out as if of its own volition.

"Yes, Gideon. Bishop Ezekiel has allowed walkies and even telephones in our office. You might have seen one on my desk." She was on a roll now, challenging him and mocking him in even measure. Pointing toward the single light mounted on the ceiling, she added, "Believe it or not, we're even allowed to have electricity because it's at our job."

"Okay. Whatever."

"Do you know how to work a walkie?"

"Yes, I know how to work one."

"Excellent. Problem solved." She put her Christmas hat back in the box, an abject look of longing on her face.

Shaking her head, she returned her attention to him. "Keep it on channel three. The range is good enough that you should be able to reach me anywhere on the property."

"Why don't we just purchase cell phones?" He meant it as a barb, irritated at her overall attitude—irritated at himself, if he were being honest.

"We could," she admitted, ushering him out of the supply closet and toward her office. "But cell phones come with a monthly payment for the service. These don't."

He was still standing by the closet door. Becca had continued down the hall. Now she turned, raised the walkie to her mouth and pushed the button. The device in his hand crackled with her amused voice. "How about we go and clear up the feed order?"

That particular issue was resolved with one call, but unfortunately, Gideon's problems didn't end there. The day literally went downhill. His quality checks resulted in some very disgruntled managers. He'd pointed out that the visitor restrooms needed more hand soap and paper towels, the livestock barn had stalls that hadn't been mucked out, and the auction restaurant had sticky menus.

"Yes, but how did you say those things?" Becca asked when they debriefed that afternoon.

"How did I *say* it?"

"What was your tone of voice?"

"I don't know what my tone of voice was."

"Probably the one you're using now, which isn't... well, it isn't pleasant."

Gideon had thrown up his hands at that.

"Seriously?"

"Yes, Gideon. Maybe they were in the process of

getting to those things. Maybe you could have complimented something they did before you criticized what they hadn't finished yet."

He'd cradled his head in his hands at that point.

"Headache?"

"A-yup."

"No worries. It'll get better."

But Tuesday was no better. It rained, so even though the market was open, crowds were down. Becca and Gideon were able to stay in the office and tackle paperwork. He tried to focus, but honestly, he probably only heard half of what Becca said. He didn't like being in the small office. The sound of rain on the roof reminded him that normally he'd be working in the barn on a rainy day. Sharing the small space made him uncomfortable. He could smell whatever shampoo Becca used. He had to listen to her humming Christmas songs, and she had a habit of glancing up and smiling at him. He already spent too much of his time away from the market thinking about Becca Yoder and her words of wisdom; he did not need to be confined in a closet-sized office with her all day.

Wednesday was once again market day, and if anything, the crowds seemed larger than the week before. He'd chosen to spend his time covering the green parking lot and adjacent vendor stalls. This included the bus drop-off and pickup. It seemed to Gideon that there was a continuous stream of Amish and *Englisch* exiting the buses. The line of cars entering the parking lot stretched down the road. He'd skipped lunch trying to resolve a disagreement between vendors in booths 621 and 622. The result had been two unhappy vendors and a worsening of his mood—something he hadn't thought possible.

By the time Becca called it a day and left, Gideon

was ready to crawl onto the last bus and see how far it would take him. He had a pounding headache and a grumbling stomach, and he felt as if his life was spiraling out of control.

This situation simply was not acceptable.

Becca had been right about one thing—he did make choices, even if it was to go along with other people's choices.

It was time that he stop complaining and take charge of his own life. It was time that he stood up to his parents. He stared at the phone on her desk, pulled in a deep breath and picked up the receiver.

Chapter Four

Becca didn't mean to eavesdrop. She'd caught up with Gideon at the bus pickup area, seen the sour look on his face and suggested they call it a day. Then she'd made one more round of the vendor stalls before heading back to her *dat*'s office. Her *dat* hadn't been quite ready to go, so she'd popped back over to her office to work through twenty minutes of paperwork. She stopped outside the door upon hearing Gideon's voice. She'd thought he'd left.

Why was he still here?

Who was he talking to?

It didn't take long for her to figure out he was arguing with his parents. If anything, his Texas accent was more pronounced, and at times he even raised his voice.

"*Ya*, I know what we agreed to, but you don't understand." There was a pause, and then he said in a quieter, more Amish tone of voice, "I'm not *gut* at this. I don't belong here. It's unlike anything you can imagine, *Dat*. There are more *Englischers* in one day here at the market than you or I would see in a year. And the Amish—

I'm not even sure they *are* Amish, they act so much like the *Englisch*."

That was rather a rude thing to say, in Becca's opinion. She considered herself very Amish. Besides, what did that even mean?

There was a pause; then Gideon said, "I didn't say I was judging. I said I don't fit here. This is not the right position for me."

There was another pause, a longer one this time.

She had to press her ear against the door to hear Gideon's response: "*Ya. Ya*, of course, but—" followed by another long pause.

She wished she could hear what his parents were saying. She suspected they were on her side in this particular situation.

The nerve of the guy.

He was trying to quit on her.

She couldn't believe it.

He'd been here a week, and he was already throwing in the towel. It made her so mad that she thought her *kapp* might pop off her head. She was probably focused on that, on her anger, and that was why she didn't hear him end the call. When he pulled the door open, she practically fell into the office.

He scowled down at her. "Eavesdropping? Seriously?"

But she was too upset to be embarrassed. It was time that she set Gideon straight about a few things, and he was going to listen. He'd promised them ninety days, and one way or another, she was going to hold him to it.

"You were calling home. I can't believe you were calling home."

"You can dock me for the long-distance charges." He

flapped a hand at the phone and scowled at her again. Then, in three long strides, he was out of the office.

Becca stood there with her mouth hanging open.

She couldn't believe this was happening. Her future was evaporating before her eyes—like a cloud dissipating on a summer day. She heard Gideon's work boots on the stairs, heading down, heading out, heading to his buggy.

She had to go after him!

Careful to close the door gently behind her so as not to alert her *dat* to anything that was going on, she hurried after Gideon. He had the advantage of a longer stride and an intense desire to get away from her. Becca broke into a jog, smiling and waving at vendors as she passed their booths. She popped out of the line of stalls only a few yards from the employee buggy-parking area.

Gideon had already hitched up Nathan's horse and was about to climb into the buggy.

Becca broke into a sprint.

She arrived next to his buggy, gasping and holding her hand against the stitch in her side. "Wait. Stop. Don't go."

"No worries, Becca. I'm not planning on driving Nathan's horse and buggy back to Texas."

The expression on his face held so much misery that she almost took pity on him. Almost. He was her ticket out of here. He needed to buck up and do his job.

"Just…come out of the buggy for a second."

"Why?"

"Because we need to talk."

"Why?"

"Because my future depends on what you do." She wasn't sure she should have said that. She had no idea if it was a good thing or a bad thing to be so brutally honest.

But then, what did she have to lose? This guy was probably going to catch the morning bus back to Texas. He'd arrive back before the bluebonnets turned into paintbrushes. "Just please—just get out for a minute."

He sighed heavily, then set the brake on the buggy and climbed out.

Becca moved to scratch the gelding behind his ears. Samson—that was the horse's name. Nathan's wife had named the animal when they'd purchased it. Becca had still been in school at the time. She could remember the smile on Mary Troyer's face the next Sunday, when she'd caught Becca feeding the horse a carrot. "He's a beautiful boy, *ya?*" And all these years later, he still was.

She knew those kinds of stories about everyone in her community. They were like a big family to her. But she knew very little about the man standing in front of her. And he knew very little about her.

She started with the obvious. "You can't go."

"You want to travel. You have plans. I'm aware."

"It's more than that."

"Just to be clear, I have dreams, too, and they don't involve an outdoor market or a town with thirty-five thousand people."

"I've applied to join an MDS work crew."

He looked at her as if she'd spoken in a foreign language.

"Mennonite Disaster Services—they work all over the country and—"

"I know who MDS is. Why would you join a work crew?"

"Because I want to help, and—"

"And you want to travel."

"Ya." She tried to think back to first meeting Gideon.

What could she have done differently? How had they ended up here...with her chasing him across a parking lot? "There aren't a lot of opportunities to travel far from home if you're a single Amish woman. I could teach, but then I'd be forced to stay in each place an entire year, and that seemed...well, it seemed a bit long."

Gideon stuck his hands in his pockets and studied her a moment, then walked over to the edge of the parking area and stared out across the market. Finally, he turned to her and said, "You can't go unless I stay."

"Pretty much."

"I knew you wanted out of here, but I figured you were going to live with a family member or something. It never occurred to me that you'd be joining MDS."

"They do amazing work."

"I'm aware. There have been MDS crews in Texas for quite a few years. First because of flooding. Then rebuilding houses in Bastrop, where there was a large wildfire. And finally, down at the coast, after a hurricane destroyed entire neighborhoods. Not that far from where I live, actually...where I *lived*."

Changing to past tense seemed to cause him a great deal of misery.

"So you understand it's important work."

"I do, but I'm sorry. I'm just having trouble catching up here. You've applied for a permanent position with them?"

"*Ya.* I don't even know what I'll be doing. My job could be cooking or cleaning or putting up drywall. And I don't care about that—not really. Volunteering means I'll be helping other people, and it'll give me a chance to see somewhere different." She sounded pathetic even to her own ears. She sounded like a child.

She stared at Samson, focused on rubbing behind his ears, focused on blinking away the tears that were threatening to fall.

Gideon stepped closer, reached into his pocket and pulled out a peppermint for the horse. Slowly, he unwrapped it, then offered it to Samson.

"It's commendable of you to agree to such a thing." His voice was soft and thoughtful.

He no longer seemed angry, and that surprised her. Was he actually considering this situation from her point of view? Was he even able to do that?

"That's quite a sacrifice to make."

Becca shook her head so hard that her *kapp* slipped a bit. She straightened it, then said, "It's not a sacrifice—let's be clear on that. I should be paying them."

"Because it's an escape for you."

"A way for me to be somewhere else and have all my expenses paid. They'll provide a place for me to stay and food for me to eat. They even supply whatever tools you need."

"But you work for free."

"Sure. I know." Her voice grew softer, more contemplative. She'd dreamed of this for so long that it had become like a reality—a life already lived and one that she might revisit soon. In her daydreams, she'd actually seen herself working on some person's house that had been ravaged and made unlivable by floodwater, or whipped away by a tornado, or burned to the ground by a fire. She'd envisioned each of those scenarios many times.

She'd even thought of being away at Christmas, of receiving a box of gifts from her family—small, homemade things, but oh, how she would treasure each one.

She'd worked herself into feeling quite unsettled over that particular daydream.

Gideon shifted his weight to his left foot, then his right—almost as if he was weighing her responses to his questions. "Why do you hate it here so much?"

"Ha. That's a funny question, coming from the guy who can't wait to get away."

"There's nothing wrong with the market, or this town, or even Indiana."

"Nothing except it's not your home."

"Correct."

She pressed her cheek against Samson's neck, then turned, walked over to an adjacent park bench and flopped down on it. "What a pickle."

Gideon looped Samson's reins over the hitching post, then joined Becca on the bench. "Yup."

"I didn't mean to eavesdrop."

"Right."

"I didn't. I'm many things, but I am not a snoop."

"So how did you happen to be pressing your ear against the closed office door?"

"I came back to do some paperwork until my *dat* was ready to leave, and when I heard you...well, I didn't want to walk in and interrupt. Then you started shouting, and it wasn't too hard to figure out the other side of the conversation. But I'm sorry. I should have walked away. It was wrong to stand there and listen to a private conversation."

"Apology accepted."

She sat up straighter and looked him directly in the eyes. He had pretty blue eyes. It was just that they were usually overshadowed by a frowning face. He wasn't frowning now, though. His expression was thoughtful.

"Seriously? You're not going to stay mad for the next day or week or however long you're here?"

Gideon shrugged. "I may be a bit of a grump—and yes, I did holler at my *dat*, which I'll be apologizing for in my letter home tonight—but I don't hold a grudge."

"Danki."

"Gem gschehne."

She almost laughed. They sounded like two normal people having a normal conversation. In that moment, she realized they'd been at odds with one another since the moment they'd met in her *dat*'s office. Had that been only a week ago? It seemed as if they'd been locked in battle for a much longer period of time.

"I haven't been much of a friend," she confessed. "I've been looking at you as my ticket out of here, and when you didn't line up with my plans...well, my reaction was as bad as your hollering."

"Why is it that I can see you stomping your foot, but it's harder to picture you raising your voice?"

She rolled her eyes. "You're not wrong."

"Maybe we should try again." He held out his hand in a very *Englisch* way, causing her to laugh. "My name's Gideon Fisher. Nice to meet you."

Slipping her hand into his, she tried to match his light tone. "And I'm Becca Yoder, assistant manager for this fine outdoor market. It would seem that's a title I'm going to keep."

Their eyes locked, and her hand slipped from his.

Gideon cleared his throat and looked away. "Surely, we can think of some solution that would work for you and for me."

"I don't see how."

Gideon stood, then reached out a hand and pulled

Becca to her feet. "I need some time away from here. Some time to think. How about we talk about this tomorrow morning?"

"Okay."

"Meet you at JoJo's Pretzels? Eighty thirty?"

"I can't believe you know where JoJo's is."

"Been there three times already." He waited for her to nod in agreement; then, without another word, he unwrapped Samson's reins, climbed into the buggy and drove away.

Leaving Becca to wonder what they could possibly have to talk about and how this would end in any way that wouldn't break her heart.

Gideon spent that evening working in Nathan's barn. First, he mucked out Samson's stall; then he spread fresh hay, filled the gelding's oat bucket and made sure there was fresh water. When he'd finished those chores, he found a piece of discarded wood, sat on an old bench and began whittling.

Nathan found him there an hour later.

"Didn't realize you were a whittler. If I'm not mistaken, that's a fine reproduction of Samson."

Gideon stared down at the piece of wood. He hadn't realized what he'd been doing, what he'd been creating. "It calms me."

"Want to talk about what you need calming from?"

Gideon shrugged, then glanced up and met Nathan's gaze. He didn't know the man well yet, but he had a pleasant personality. He didn't gossip about the neighbors whose goats constantly escaped into their pasture, often eating some of his crop before anyone realized they were in the wrong place. He also didn't complain, though it was plain that his arthritis made grasping his coffee cup difficult in the mornings.

Now he picked up a piece of sandpaper and began working on a four-foot piece of maple wood with a circumference of about six inches.

"Are you making a walking stick?"

"*Ya.* I hear tourists love Amish-made items." He winked at Gideon. "Though it would be more accurate to say that *Gotte* made this piece of wood. I'm merely caring for it."

They sat silently for a while as Gideon whittled and Nathan sanded. It helped, the silence did. Helped his emotions to calm and his mind to line up the questions he needed answers to.

Whittling had always come easy to him. He enjoyed being alone and allowing the silence around him to soothe his soul. The whittling was like a gift and one of the few things that set him apart from his eight siblings, whom he'd been born in the middle of. Thinking of his *bruders* and *schweschdern*, he remembered the time his bishop had spoken to him about middle-child syndrome.

The bishop had explained that the idea was that middle children often felt as if they didn't fit in with the older group or the younger group. They felt caught in the middle. At the time, Gideon had laughed and assured the bishop that he was fine. He could remember being angry about it afterward, though. Why did the bishop and his parents and even his siblings assume there was something wrong with him? Maybe there was something wrong with everyone else.

Or maybe his bishop had been onto something, because even here, even fourteen hundred miles from home, he still felt as if he didn't quite fit.

Turning the wood over in his hands, he had the sensation that someone had handed it to him fully carved. He had very little to do with it. What was it Nathan had said? *Gotte made this... I'm merely caring for it.* Those words, they gave Gideon the courage to speak to Nathan. He cleared his throat, but he didn't look up. He kept his eyes on the horse that was taking shape.

He explained about his parents, how they'd wanted him to come to Indiana. How they had arranged the job at Amos Yoder's market. He told the old man how uncomfortable he was there, how different it was from farming in a rural Texas community. And he even spoke of Becca and how his emotions around her confounded him.

"Can't say as I've ever reacted to a woman that way before," he admitted. "One moment, I'm so aggravated at her that I'm sure the buttons on my suspenders are going to pop off. The next, I'm laughing at something she said or did."

When he'd finished baring his soul, the old man didn't offer any advice, which was a point in his favor. Instead, he simply nodded as if everything that Gideon had said made sense.

It didn't make sense. Even he could admit that.

"No words of advice?"

"Oh. I wasn't sure you wanted any." Nathan grinned as he wiped the walking stick clean with an old cotton cloth. Then he reached for a bottle of linseed oil, splashed a little of it onto another cotton cloth and began rubbing the oil into the wood. The process was mesmerizing. It was like watching a watercolor painting come to life. The grain of the wood began to shine, and the beauty of the wood became apparent to Gideon, even from a distance of three feet.

"Well, I wouldn't turn down any advice. Plainly, I'm at a loss as to what to do."

"About which thing?"

"Any of them."

"Ah." And still Nathan didn't offer any words of instruction.

Gideon felt like laughing. How many times had his parents offered advice, or his older *bruders*? He'd always rolled his eyes and wished they'd stop talking, wished they'd stop assuming they understood what he was going through.

"How can anyone really understand what someone else is going through?" Nathan's words so closely mirrored Gideon's thoughts that he was taken aback.

"Pardon?"

"What I mean is, I've been on this Earth a long time. Eighty-seven years, to be exact. But I can't say that I've had to deal with the things you're struggling with now. My life was very different from yours." He continued rubbing the oil into the wood, turning the walking stick this way and that.

Gideon returned to his whittling, shaping the horse's ears and eyes.

"Life passes so fast, like a runaway horse pulling a buggy." Nathan smiled, though he didn't look up. "That happened to me once. I thought I'd broken the horse—but truthfully, I didn't want to spend any more time training it. So I harnessed it to an old buggy of my *dat*'s. Before you could say *Shipshewana*, that horse and my *dat*'s buggy were down the lane and dashing across the fields, trampling a good bit of corn."

The old man's voice was soft as the night, almost

lyrical. Gideon found himself easily picturing the runaway horse.

"We called him Geronimo." Nathan looked up now and smiled. He held out his hand—wrinkled by time, veins prominently close to the surface, age spots spread across his skin like a tan. He held out his hand and then motioned toward himself as if to welcome the horse home.

He laughed, dropping his hand. "He was a fine horse, and I miss him still. I really do."

Gideon understood that the horse wasn't the only thing Nathan was missing. How would it feel to be eighty-seven and to have the bulk of your life behind you?

Nathan stood, put the linseed oil back on the shelf, carefully folded the cloths he had used and then set the walking stick next to the others he had worked on.

Gideon thought that was that. He thought Nathan had no wisdom to share, only feelings for what had been lost.

Nathan didn't leave, though. He sat next to Gideon on the bench, his palms pressed together as if in prayer. Somehow, sitting that way—sitting shoulder to shoulder—made listening easier for Gideon.

"I can't tell you what job to take or not take, whether to follow your parents' wishes, what your feelings for Becca might be. I can't tell you any of those things, my friend."

Gideon tried for a laugh, but it came out as more of a croak. His hands stilled on the piece of wood. His heart, his very soul, seemed both wary and eager to hear something Nathan hadn't yet said.

"I can tell you that eighty-seven years pass like a spring storm—here and then suddenly gone. Not so long ago, I was a young scholar, carrying my lunch pail to the first day of school. Then I blinked and I was twenty-five, nervous and in love and worried that Mary would say no to my suggestion that we marry." He kneaded his left hand with the right, attempting to ease the tightness there. "And then it seemed as if the very next moment, I was sitting beside her bed, praying for *Gotte*'s mercy, praying for a few more days."

We're born, we fall in love, and then we die? Yikes.

Was that Nathan's idea of a pep talk?

But Nathan wasn't finished. He stood, then placed his hand on Gideon's back. "Give love when you can, respect when you should and always—*always*—put first things first."

Gideon sat there a long time after Nathan left, no longer working on the piece of wood, not even aware of the passage of time. When he finally went into the house, Nathan was already in his room with the door closed, down for the night, asleep—he assumed.

Sleep didn't come so easily for Gideon. He lay in his bed, stared at the ceiling, tossed and turned. He worried and wondered and thought of—then discarded—several ideas.

Nothing was as simple as he'd pretended it to be. Becca wasn't a selfish young woman wanting to escape the confines of a too-close family.

She wanted to work on a mission trip.

She wanted to dedicate a portion of her life to helping others.

And what did he want? He wanted to have the life he'd always had, to be left alone, to work the fields and not have to deal with people or commitment or change.

That realization didn't help him feel any better. He

might be selfish, but didn't he have a right to live the life of his choosing?

How could they both have what they wanted?

He remembered Nathan's words. And when it seemed about time for the rooster to crow, when he was certain that he'd worried the night away without a moment of rest to show for it, he finally slipped into an uneasy slumber.

Chapter Five

Gideon was still hearing Nathan's words as he trudged into the Davis Mercantile the next morning.

Give love when you can. What did that even mean? He had a feeling Nathan wasn't referring to romantic love, though Gideon wasn't at all sure that he felt anything even close to love for Becca. He barely knew her. And she could be so aggravating.

Maybe Nathan had meant it in a *love your neighbor* sense.

He supposed he could work with that.

Respect when you should. He was pretty sure that applied to his parents. He understood all too well what that meant. If you respected someone, then you followed their lead where possible. You certainly shouldn't break a promise to someone you respected. You shouldn't break a promise to anyone.

Always put first things first. Gideon had absolutely no idea what that meant.

He needed coffee.

He made his way over to the line at JoJo's. The little eatery was a cheerful-looking place, with lots of wooden beams and red-painted walls. The booths sported black-and-white tabletops with red seats. It gave him the impression of stepping back in time to an old-fashioned drugstore. Some of the small towns in Texas still had those. He'd yet to come here when there weren't half a dozen people in line—Amish and *Englisch*. The smell of the freshly made pretzels made his stomach grumble.

Where was Becca? He looked across the room and finally spied her in the adjacent coffee shop, trying to get his attention. He waved, then ordered his pretzel—a cinnamon sugar, which at this point was his absolute favorite.

He carried the basket over to where Becca sat—looking disturbingly perky, fresh, well rested.

"I ordered your coffee—no cream, two sugars."

"How did you know that?"

"Seriously? You've drank coffee at every lunch we've had together, which has been every day you've worked at the market." She raised her cup and took a long sip, closing her eyes in appreciation. "Coffee is the primary ingredient of every breakfast. In fact, some days, coffee is the sole ingredient of breakfast."

"You're awfully bright and sunny this morning." It came out crabbier than he intended.

"I guess. There's no sense in moping around."

"You're making me think the real Becca has been kidnapped and a kinder, gentler Becca put in her place."

"Have I been that bad?"

Instead of answering, he broke off a piece of the warm pretzel and popped the treat into his mouth. It was impossible to be irritated at anyone with a bite of JoJo's cinnamon-sugar pretzel in your mouth. As Becca watched him, he tried to remember what he was going to say to her, but all he could think about was how pretty she looked.

Her *kapp* was freshly starched and pinned back an inch or so from her hairline. Becca's hair was a mystery to Gideon. Sometimes he thought it was blond, but other times, he was sure it was brown. It sort of changed according to the light. Was that even possible? She was wearing a light green dress that made him think of spring in Texas.

"You should see this place at Christmas."

He didn't even try to hold in the groan. "Not that again."

She leaned forward, her eyes sparkling. "They put green and red sprinkles on the whipped cream, there's a Christmas tree over in that corner, and small white lights are strung all over the room. They even hire one of the high school students to paint a Christmas scene on the windows. It's very special."

Gideon stared at her. He had honestly never met anyone quite like Becca Yoder.

"Why are you looking at me that way? Do I have..." She reached for a napkin. "Is there whipped cream on my face?"

He dropped his gaze to his coffee, trying to make a coherent sentence out of the things he needed to tell her.

She blotted at her face, then cocked her head. "What? It's plain you have something to say. Don't keep me waiting over here. If you're leaving today, I need to put an ad in the paper, though I'm not sure how much good that will do since the season has already begun and—"

"I'm not leaving today."

"Oh." She blinked several times. "That's *gut.*"

Love. Respect. First things first.

Gideon's mind was suddenly blank—as blank as a school chalkboard that had been recently cleaned.

"Whatever you're about to say must be terrible. Is it terrible? I can take it. I gave myself a stern lecture last night."

Gideon looked down at his basket. The pretzel was gone. He'd already eaten the entire thing? Pushing the basket away, he sipped the coffee. It was perfect—two sugars, no cream. He needed to get this conversation over with.

"I'm not leaving today," he repeated. Then, at the look of excitement on her face, he quickly added, "But my parents agreed to a thirty-day trial period instead of ninety."

"Thirty days?"

"Since I've already been here a week, that gives us about…"

"Twenty-three more days, but that's only three weeks."

"I realize it's inconvenient."

"*Inconvenient?* It's a disaster." She narrowed her eyes and stared at a spot over his left shoulder.

"Give me a little credit here. At least I'm willing to stay for thirty days. If you still want me to."

"Of course I want you to. What good does it do me for you to leave now?" She slumped back into her chair.

He waited.

Finally, she said, "Okay. Fine. I can work with that."

"Work with what?"

"Thirty days. I always did think a ninety-day trial period was too long."

"You did?"

"It was *Dat*'s idea. Once his mind is made up, you might as well try to give a cat a bath."

"I don't have a cat."

"I'm just saying it would be easier than changing his mind. By the way, you're the one telling him of the adjustment in your plans. Make sure I'm on the other side of the market or something."

"You're taking this awfully well."

"Not really." She leaned forward and rested her forehead against the table, then abruptly sat up straight. "Actually, this is my fault. I shouldn't have let finding my replacement be a condition for my leaving. That's between me and *Dat*, and I will be speaking to him about it. In the meantime, who knows, maybe our little market will grow on you."

"Huh."

"Exactly what I was thinking."

They collected their trash and dropped it into a receptacle, then stepped out into a beautiful May morning. Horses clip-clopped down the road next to *Englisch* cars. Shop owners swept the front of their sidewalks and turned Closed signs to Open.

"I have to admit, the cool mornings here are nice."

Becca stumbled back in mock surprise.

"What?"

"You said something nice about Indiana. Maybe I misheard you. Say it again."

Instead of indulging her, he asked, "Did you walk here from the market?"

"Of course."

"Then come on. I'll give you a ride back to work."

"Only if you let me drive."

"Let you *drive*?"

"I know how to drive a horse and buggy. We have an old mare named Oreo, who I'm quite good with, and a young mare named Peanut, who is the sweetest thing you could ask for in a buggy horse."

"Didn't realize a horse could be sweet."

"Plus, Samson and I just happen to be old friends."

"Is that so?"

"It is." She smirked back over her shoulder as she hurried toward Nathan's buggy. He didn't try to match her pace, and he only pretended to be afraid when she climbed up into the driver's seat.

He had a feeling that little Becca Yoder could do anything she put her mind to—drive a horse and buggy, manage an outdoor market, hang drywall in a stranger's home. The only question he had was why she'd given in to his shortened trial period so easily.

It seemed to him that Becca was up to something, and he was pretty sure that he would find out soon enough what that something was.

Becca dropped into a rocker on the back porch and stared up at Eunice, who was perched on top of a ladder, installing the solar ceiling fan. It looked like an ordinary fan to Becca, much like those on the porch of their *Englisch* neighbors.

"Do you need help with that?"

Eunice was holding the fan up with one hand and reaching for an electrical wire with the other. The wire ran across the ceiling of the porch to the edge of the roof overhang, where a small solar panel was mounted. As Eunice reached for the wire, the ladder began to tip. Becca popped out of her chair just in time to hold it steady.

"Danki," Eunice said. "That was close."

"You shouldn't be doing these things alone." That was what Becca said, but what she thought was that her *schweschder* shouldn't be doing these things at all.

"Thought I could reach it." Eunice was mumbling because she was holding a screwdriver in her mouth. "One more second."

Something clicked into something else, and then Eunice grinned down at her. "That should do it." She scampered down the ladder and walked over to a switch she'd screwed into the wall of the porch.

"Ready?"

"I guess." But Becca took several big steps back and away from the contraption, in case it fell or sent down showers of sparks when Eunice hit the button.

She hit the button.

No falling parts.

No sparks.

Just the soft whir of a fan.

"It works."

"Don't sound so surprised."

"I *am* surprised."

"Why would you be? I actually know what I'm doing."

"Now you do, apparently. But you didn't know what you were doing the time you tried to hook a solar pump to the horses' water trough."

"I was younger then."

"It was last fall."

"And I learned from my mistake. You have to admit, the fan is nice."

"It is at that."

They both sat in the rockers, smiling at one another. Simultaneously, they reached for a glass of iced tea that

Becca had brought out earlier. Laughing, they clinked the glasses together. It felt silly and young and carefree.

Becca wanted to be silly and young and carefree.

She sighed heavily, the sigh of a much older person—a serious, responsible, mature person.

"Problems at the market?"

"How did you guess?"

"You always make that face when there's problems at the market."

"What face?"

"The one you're… never mind. So, what's the problem?"

"In a word—Gideon."

"Hmm. Wish I could help, sis, but I know nothing about guys."

"Half the time, you have your head stuck inside a piece of machinery you're working on with guys."

"Well, sure, but that's different because we're working."

"You spend more time with Zeb Mast than you do with your own family."

"I guess, but Zeb is like a *bruder*. I don't think whatever problem you're having with Gideon is like that."

"It isn't. My problem with Gideon is that he's stubborn and homesick, and he's a constant worrier. It's enough to drive you a little *narrisch*."

"So it isn't his work ethic?"

"Nein." She explained about eavesdropping on his phone call, about his decision to stay thirty days but not the agreed-upon ninety.

"He can do the work?"

"Ya, sure. Doesn't take a genius." Becca stared up at the whirring fan. "He works hard. If he'd relax around

the vendors, he'd get along better with them. He's a bit tense, you know?"

"Like a fish out of water."

"Exactly."

"A horse in the city."

"I guess."

"An Amish girl on a cruise ship."

They both laughed, and then Becca said, "Okay. Enough with the analogies." She did feel better, though. Eunice always made her feel better because Eunice saw things simply.

Becca supposed if you were adept at working with machines, then life might seem less complicated. She didn't understand mechanical things at all. If anything broke at the market, she called maintenance. If anything broke at home, she called Eunice. Becca supposed if you learned how to rig up one solar ceiling fan, you could rig up a dozen. Machines didn't complicate things with feelings. "Tell me how you would fix this if it were a solar panel."

"Solar panel?"

"Or whatever. Logically, how would you fix this? Because it's looking more and more like I won't get out of here until next year, and that's sort of breaking my heart."

"I'm sorry, sis."

"Not your fault."

"True." Eunice pressed her fingertips together and studied something in the distance. Finally, she turned to Becca. "Okay. So you have two problems."

"Only two?"

Eunice retrieved a tape measure from the pocket of her apron and pulled out the tab, stretching the tape.

She let it go—*thwack*—then pulled it out and let it go again. *Thwack.*

Becca snatched it out of her hands and sat back with a smile. "You were saying?"

"Goodness, you're jumpy. I think better when I have something in my hands."

"And I'll return this when you solve my problems." Becca wiggled the tape measure back and forth. "You know you want it."

Eunice rolled her eyes.

"You were saying I have two problems."

"Right. One is Gideon—obviously."

"Obviously."

"And the other is *Dat.*"

"True enough."

"Start with *Dat.* Tell him you'd like to renegotiate."

"Okay." Becca turned the tape measure over and over in her hand. Finally, she admitted, "I don't know how to do that."

"Meet him halfway. Agree to stay in your current position until spring, but insist that your leaving not be contingent on finding a replacement. Let's be honest. There are a dozen guys here in Shipshe who could do that job and do it well."

"I was thinking the same thing."

"So *Dat* was procrastinating. He was putting off your leaving because he was worried about you."

"Hmm." Could it be that simple? Maybe she had been overthinking this.

"Tell him you appreciate his worry but that you're old enough to make your own decisions. Meet him halfway. Stay until spring, but no longer."

Becca sighed. Eunice was right. This wasn't an either/

or situation. It wasn't a matter of her having the things she wanted in life right this minute or never having them. She wasn't a child, and she could handle change with maturity. So what if she wanted to kick a buggy tire? She didn't have to respond that way.

"I don't want to stay until spring, but it wouldn't be the end of the world." She rather liked the idea of spending one last Christmas at home. Yes, she had envisioned what it would be like in Florida or Tennessee or even California, but she wouldn't mind one more Indiana Christmas. "I suppose spring would be the worst case. There's still a possibility—albeit a slim one—that Gideon will serve his thirty days and decide to stay."

Eunice shrugged as if to say *maybe that could happen, but don't count on it.*

Becca would have to find a way to convince Gideon that he could make a home and be happy in Shipshe. She'd have to change his mind that Texas was the only place he could truly be content.

"Problem number two is a bit trickier." Eunice took another sip of tea.

"Gideon."

"What are some things he likes?"

"Texas. He likes everything about Texas. He goes on and on and on about the Lone Star state."

"Such as what?"

"Crops, wildflowers, droughts…"

"Who likes a drought?"

"Scorching heat, cattle, hard work, rodeos…"

"Too bad our rodeo isn't until November." Eunice snapped her fingers, then leaned forward and grabbed her tape measure out of Becca's hands. "That's it."

"What's it?"

"Take him to the buggy races this weekend. It's not a rodeo, but it's close enough."

"I don't want to take him to the buggy races. I spend all week with him. The last thing I want to do is spend Saturday with him too."

"Then find another girl to do it." Eunice grinned at her as if she'd dropped a Christmas package into her lap. "Maybe he just needs to see the fun side of our little community."

"He thinks our community is huge."

"Convince him otherwise." Eunice stood and stretched, sending a satisfied glance toward the ceiling fan. "I better go wash up. Wouldn't want to arrive at the dinner table with grease on my hands."

"You always show up with grease on your hands…" But Becca was talking to herself. Eunice had already gone inside.

Actually, her *schweschder*'s idea made sense.

Gideon was homesick because he hadn't met anyone here, and he hadn't met anyone because he was too homesick to be sociable. If she invited him to the buggy races, he'd get out of his own head for a few minutes. He also might meet some people…some friends—a girlfriend, even.

If Gideon had a girlfriend, he'd stay.

Eunice was a genius!

Now all Becca had to do was convince Gideon to go with her Saturday and then make sure the right girls were also in attendance. She'd start a list. Then she'd go down to the phone shack and place a few calls. Let the Amish grapevine do the work for her.

And she'd have that talk with her *dat*. Because if a day at the buggy races didn't work—and she fully realized it was a long shot—then she would rather not stay another nine months. There had to be a quicker way to end her servitude. Maybe she could go on a new year's mission. That was only six months away.

But she didn't want to go in March or even in January. Her mind—and her heart—kept wavering back and forth. On the one hand, she knew that having to wait wouldn't be the end of her dreams. On the other hand, she was terribly impatient to go. She wanted to leave in August like she'd planned. If she played her cards right, that still might be possible.

Chapter Six

Gideon couldn't believe that he'd agreed to accompany Becca to the buggy races. Buggy races? Who had time for such silliness? In Texas, you worked six days a week and rested on Sunday. It was the only way to make a living as a farmer.

But he wasn't a farmer anymore.

He was an assistant manager, and there was nothing to manage because the market was closed on weekends.

Even Nathan had liked the idea. "I'm going to play horseshoes at the fairgrounds. You can drop me off."

Which was how he found himself driving the buggy, Becca by his side, Becca's youngest *schweschder* and Nathan in the back seat. The two of them were getting along as if they'd known each other all their lives. When he muttered as much to Becca, she said, "They have. Well, all of Ada's life, obviously. Not all of Nathan's life."

Gideon had never met anyone like Ada. She was always in a good mood—bouncy, even—and very chatty. She threw her arms around in a dramatic fashion when she talked, and she seemed to get along with everyone. Girls like that were a mystery to him, and not in a good

way. They made him feel a bit dour and old. At least with
Becca, he could hold a serious conversation without her
changing direction several times.

He shared as much with Becca, in a low voice, and
to his surprise she nodded in agreement. "Ada has the
energy of three of us. We keep thinking that she'll out-
grow it."

"I guess I haven't really known that many girls. My
family is mostly guys."

"No girls at all?" Becca stared at him curiously.

"My *mamm*, of course. And I have one *schweschder*.
Deborah's the youngest—only twenty-four. She married a year ago and is already expecting her first *boppli*. I guess girls marry pretty young in our community."

"Around here, girls marry much younger than that. I
have several friends who married as soon as they turned
eighteen. Makes me feel like an old maid some days. I'm
twenty-four—"

"Same age as Deborah."

"Right, and I have no intention of marrying this year
or next. I'm going to—"

"Travel. I know. You've mentioned it."

Laughter spilled from the back seat.

"What's so funny back there?" Becca turned in her
seat. "If you're telling jokes, I want to hear one."

"No jokes." Nathan raised his hand and smiled. "Just
life."

Ada laughed again. "Life indeed. I was telling Nathan
about the Schwartz twins and what a mess that job was
from the get-go. Two sets of twins? No thank you! And
Dat wanted me to start working at Yoder's today, but I
told him that all work and no play makes Jack a bull boy."

Gideon glanced at Becca, then over his shoulder at

Ada. A bull boy? He had no idea what that was. Ada must have noticed his look of confusion because she draped her arms over the seat and stuck her head in between him and Becca. "Haven't you ever heard that one?"

Becca was covering her face with her hands, laughing at something.

"It means Jack needs time off. Or he'll get angry like a bull. A bull boy. Get it?"

"I don't think that's how it goes."

"Oh, I'm sure it is." Ada flopped back against her seat. "I don't want to be a bull boy or bull girl. It's important to have fun sometimes."

Becca finally managed to get her laughter under control. "It's an Ada-ism."

"A what?"

"An Ada-ism. Ada loves to quote sayings, but she usually gets them wrong."

"Don't start with me, Becca, because this time I'm pretty sure I'm right, and I don't want to embarrass you by having to prove it. Maybe I should prove it. Nathan, what do you think?"

Fortunately for Gideon, who felt as if he had no idea what anyone was talking about, they arrived at the fairgrounds. Gideon helped Nathan out of the buggy, and he ambled off, calling out over his shoulder, "Someone here will take me home." Several of the old guys greeted Nathan as he walked toward lawn chairs that had been placed in a circle of shade. The distinct clank of horseshoes hitting a pole rang out.

Gideon had a fleeting thought to stay there, to hang out with the old guys rather than spend his free day in a crowd. One look at Becca told him that wouldn't work. She was standing up on the running board and impatiently tapping her foot. He sighed and walked around to the driver's side.

Becca directed him out of the fairgrounds, down the road and to the parking area behind the Blue Gate. The sheer number of buggies and *Englisch* cars made him nervous. Twice he jerked on the reins, certain that Samson would swerve into the path of the automobiles. Becca rolled her eyes and assured him that he was the only one nervous driving next to cars. Then she commenced humming "We Wish You a Merry Christmas."

Finally, they reached the parking area for buggies. Ada hopped out before he'd even set the brake, waving and saying she'd also find her own way home.

"Gosh. She was in a hurry to get away."

"You know how *youngies* are." Becca slipped her hand through the crook of his arm and smiled up at him.

It was a very strange thing for her to do. His face, neck and ears suddenly felt hot. Why was she looking at him that way? He'd seen farmers looking at turkeys in the same manner, usually when they were sizing up which one to have for dinner. "Why are you acting this way?"

"Acting what way?"

"What's up with you?"

"Nothing's up. Can't I take a coworker to see the buggy races without being interrogated?"

"I wasn't interrogating."

"Oh, look. There's some of our friends from church."

He felt as if he was being dragged through a crowd of *Englischers* and Amish alike. They were lined up along both sides of the road. At one end, and stretched across the street, were three lines of buggies, conspicuously missing their horses. At both ends stood two men with clipboards—one Amish, one *Englisch*.

Becca introduced Gideon to a rather large group of girls. He caught the names—Janet, Hannah, Emily, Claire and Eunice—but there was little hope that he would keep straight in his mind which name belonged to which girl. Why were they looking at him like he was a Christmas present with a bow on it? Ugh. Becca's Christmas fascination was wearing off on him. And why did Eunice look so familiar?

Wait, wasn't Eunice Becca's *schweschder*? It had to be Eunice because there was a bit of grease on her face, which Becca leaned forward and wiped off after licking her thumb. Eunice pulled away and swatted at Becca's hand; then both started laughing.

Why hadn't Eunice ridden with her *schweschder* if she was coming? All of a sudden, the crowd started cheering and clapping and jostling, and it didn't seem like a good idea to try and ask a question.

Becca moved closer, and Gideon leaned down to hear what she was saying. "The teams include four people. Two ride and two pull. When they reach the end, the buggies are turned around. At that point, riders and drivers switch places, then race back."

Which made no sense at all to him, but then the man holding the clipboard and standing at the far end raised his hand. The crowd quieted, and the other man blew a whistle. The buggies at the front of the rows took off. Spectators cheered and clapped and laughed when one of the teenage boys pulling the far-left buggy lost his hat, and someone in the crowd snatched it up, screaming, "Got it. Keep going!"

The buggies reached the end. Drivers jumped out, pullers hopped in and then they were off again. The team with the teenager who had lost his hat won, and everyone congratulated them, even the people competing against them. There was a short pause as a new group of contestants lined up, and then the race started all over again.

Gideon was surprised to hear himself laugh and find himself cheering on people he didn't know. It actually looked kind of fun. Becca leaned close and said, "If you're still here next year, you can sign up. You might even win!"

"Oh, I would win if I signed up." He didn't know why he'd said that. It sounded funny in his head, but he was afraid it sounded arrogant coming out of his mouth. Becca only smiled, then motioned to one of her friends— was it Janet or Hannah or…what were the other names?

The next thing he knew, Becca was walking away, and he was surrounded by the girls she'd introduced him to. He craned his neck, trying to see where she'd gone, but then Emily or maybe Claire asked if they had buggy races in Texas. He tried to answer, but the next race started, and his words were carried away on the light afternoon breeze.

It seemed as if one minute, he was standing there with Becca, watching buggy races, and the next, he was seated outside the local coffee shop with a table full of girls. Eunice had begged off, claiming she needed to meet someone about a solar panel. The other four girls seemed content to sit and gab. He tried to nod and laugh at the appropriate places, but he kept glancing around, looking for Becca. Where had she gone?

He was beginning to understand the *why* of her leaving, but what he didn't know was how he was supposed to find her to take her home again. He might be irritated with her—he was *absolutely* irritated with her—but he still needed to give her a ride home. Just when he thought he might have to ask one of the girls surrounding him about Becca's whereabouts, she popped out of the crowd across the street and walked toward them.

She said, "There you are," as if she had been searching for him. The grin on her face only served to provoke him more, but he wasn't about to let on…not when they had an audience. Just maybe it was time he started playing offense with little Miss Becca Yoder. He thought he knew a pretty good way to turn the tables.

Jumping out of his seat, he pulled it out and held it for her. "We were wondering about you. I bet you're exhausted. Sit here."

She looked at him as if he'd suggested she join one of the buggy-race teams.

"I'll just pop in and get you a coffee—no sugar, topped with whipped cream, right?"

"Um, sure."

He purchased a muffin, too, though it cost him another three bucks. He needed his devotion for Becca to look convincing. He needed to sell this romantic tale if he wanted the other girls to believe it. Returning to the outdoor table, he placed the coffee and muffin in front of Becca. "They had chocolate chip muffins—your favorite."

Now the other girls were throwing covert glances at one another. He was nearly there. He fetched a chair from another table and pulled it up close to Becca's. "Did you have a *gut* time looking for your *schweschder*'s gift?"

"What—"

"Ada's. You know, the one we talked about in the buggy."

"We—"

"I'm just getting to know all of Becca's *schweschdern*,

since there are so many of them." He smiled and made eye contact with each of the girls sitting around the table. "But I know how important it is to have a *gut* relationship with your girl's family."

Becca choked on the bite of muffin she'd swallowed, and he had to pat her on the back. After she had recovered her composure, he let his arm rest on the back of her chair. Two of the girls stood, claiming they just remembered somewhere they needed to be and apologizing for hurrying off. Two more lasted through his recounting their morning coffee date at JoJo's before they saw friends and dashed away, as well.

By that time, Becca was glowering at him, and Gideon was feeling pretty good about how he'd turned her little game around. He'd teach Becca to stay out of his personal life, even if he did have to create a fake relationship between them to do it.

Becca was feeling perplexed, irritated and more than a little unsettled by the time they walked back to the buggy. Gideon, on the other hand, was actually in the best mood she'd seen to date. He was actually whistling. Whistling! It made her want to dump the rest of her coffee on him.

Without speaking, they climbed up into the buggy. He released the brake and called out to Samson. Finally, Gideon glanced her way and started laughing, and she had to fight the urge to stamp her foot. It was awkward to stamp her foot while riding in a buggy, so instead she crossed her arms and gave him her sternest stare.

"Won't work, my love."

"Your *love*?"

"You started this. Don't be mad at me for turning it around on you."

"Started what?"

"Luring me to town, supposedly to see buggy races—which were quite amusing, by the way. If you'd stopped with your little plan right there, it might have worked."

"Worked?"

"*Ya.* You might have convinced me that there are advantages to such a big community. But you couldn't stop there because you are Becca, and Becca wants to win. Becca's motto should be *go big or go home*."

"I don't know what you're talking about." She did know what he was talking about. What she couldn't figure out was how he'd caught on to her plan so quickly.

"Or rather, go big so the sucker with you won't go home—back to Texas, where he belongs." There wasn't any of the normal longing in his voice. He was acting decidedly strange. The perpetual worry line on his brow was missing, and he looked relaxed driving the buggy. He didn't even startle when an *Englisch* car passed them.

Glancing at her, he asked, "Do you know where you went wrong?"

"Went wrong?"

"If it had only been one friend or two that we bumped into—" he raised his right hand to put quote marks around the word *bumped* "—I might not have caught on. But five? Five Amish girls your age who aren't married or even going steady?"

"How do you know they weren't married?"

"Because they would have been with their husband. Same thing if they'd had a boyfriend. But *nein*, they were just standing in a little group, waiting for you to walk over, leading me like a lamb to slaughter."

Becca's eyes widened, and she didn't know whether to vehemently deny his allegations or laugh. He was so pleased with himself for having figured out her plan.

Finally, she managed, "How is introducing you to friends like slaughtering a lamb?"

"And the worst part was you included your own *schweschder.*"

"I didn't even know for certain Eunice was going to be there. Yes, I asked her to, but more often than not, she gets carried away with one of her mechanical projects and forgets what she had planned to do."

"That's when I knew something was up. Why didn't she ride with us? Why didn't she go off with Ada?"

"Oh, I could barely talk her into coming to town at all, let alone running around with Ada." Becca slapped her hand over her mouth. He'd tricked her into telling more of the truth than she'd planned to share, and from the expression on his face, he knew it.

Gideon reached up and tipped his straw hat back. "So that's why she didn't stick around. I thought it was that I didn't rise to your description…"

"Why would I describe you to my friends and my *schweschder*? Besides, Eunice had already met you. As for the other girls…" She actually had spent thirty minutes describing Gideon to her *freinden* on the phone the night before.

"Eunice must have owed you something. I'm guessing she's happier at home and doesn't really like crowds."

"Then you two should have a lot in common!" Becca finally turned to face him—a little ashamed, but also feeling as if he had just proven her point. "You two are alike, and at this rate, you'll never meet anyone. Do you want to be alone until you're Nathan's age?"

"I'm so touched that you're worried about my future." He was smiling, but somehow it didn't reach his eyes.

His mood had turned again, which meant she had struck a nerve. She also knew that probably meant she should stop talking, but Becca wasn't always good at staying silent when she should.

"My *schweschder* as well as those four friends of mine are *gut* people. You'd be lucky to have a date with any one of them."

"So you admit today was a setup."

"I didn't admit anything." She turned back toward the front of the buggy, crossed her arms tightly and pretended to be deeply absorbed in watching the homes they passed.

Silence settled around them—a heavy, uncomfortable silence.

If he'd kept talking, she might have been able to hold on to her anger, her self-righteous reasoning. Instead, Gideon had grown quiet, and she found herself questioning both what she'd done and her motivation for doing so.

He pulled down her lane, then stopped in front of her house, and still he didn't speak. The problem was that there was no church meeting the next day. Becca was self-aware enough to know she'd spend every hour until Monday morning feeling bad about her little attempt to trick Gideon into dating. Best to apologize now and get it over with.

"I'm sorry."

He turned toward her, his expression revealing nothing.

"Seriously. I am, sorry. Somehow..." She worried her thumbnail, then clasped her hands in her lap. "Somehow in my head, it was justified."

"What was justified?" When she only looked at him, he added, "I need to hear you say it. If you can't say it, you're not really sorry, and then it might happen again."

"Oh, good grief. Don't flatter yourself. Okay? I don't know that many girls looking for a beau. And yes, I admit it—I tried to set you up. Is that so wrong?"

"Well, it was a little sneaky."

"Guilty. I guess."

"You guess?"

"Guilty."

"And you won't repeat it?"

"I won't."

"You promise that you won't try to throw any of your other *schweschdern* at me?"

She could sense that his anger was dissipating. She tapped a finger against her lips and looked at her home, then back at him. "Let's see. There's still Sarah, who is probably too old at twenty-eight."

"I'm twenty-eight."

"With her reputation as a runaway bride, I didn't feel right about suggesting it."

"Thank you very much."

"Eunice would actually make some man a *gut* match—that is, a man who is very secure, because Eunice would be fixing things in the barn while he's looking after the *boppli*."

Gideon laughed at that; then his expression grew more serious—almost sympathetic. "I hadn't fully understood your situation. So all the Yoder girls are available?"

"Much to my *dat*'s dismay…yes."

"What about you?"

"What about me?" Becca felt her face flame red. She'd

never been able to control a blush, so instead, she looked at the buggy's ceiling.

"Why aren't you dating?"

Before she could answer, he waved away her response. "Traveling. I know. You don't have time for a man."

"It's true." She gave him an embarrassed smile. "Bethany is a sweetheart. You'd be lucky to have her."

"Uh-huh. And don't forget Ada."

"Oh, I haven't. She's so full of energy, as you know, and gads of fun." When he didn't answer, she added, "Ada's the pet of the family. We all dote on her."

He pretended to be considering it, then leaned forward and asked, "How old is she?"

"Eighteen."

"A full ten years younger—so no, that won't work, I'm afraid."

"You're awfully picky."

"Actually, what I am is not interested." He sat back, looking smug. "*Gut* try, though."

Becca hopped out of the buggy, feeling disappointed and embarrassed and irritated all at the same time.

Gideon didn't immediately pull away, though. He sat there watching her until finally she put her hand on top of her *kapp* and said, "What?"

He grinned. "See you Monday." Calling out to Samson, he directed the horse back down the lane.

And Becca stood there, wondering what else she could do to convince Gideon Fisher that Shipshewana was the best place on Earth.

Chapter Seven

❧

June arrived and with it came an increase in the size of the crowds at the market. Summer was Becca's favorite time of year. She loved not needing to wear a sweater, working in the garden in the afternoon and sitting on the front porch each evening. Northern Indiana was a thing of beauty in June—with the quilt gardens ablaze with color and the wildflowers flourishing and the crops stretching as far as she could see. The leaves on the trees were a green so bright, it almost hurt her eyes to stare at them.

So why was she feeling melancholy?

While it was true that Gideon's thirty-day-countdown clock was ticking, Becca had pretty much accepted her fate. She'd come to terms with the idea that it wasn't the end of the world if she didn't leave until the new year or even spring. She promised herself that she'd enjoy her last few months at home.

Perhaps that was why Ada's misquoted sayings were so funny.

And Sarah's mothering didn't irritate her.

Even Eunice's projects had taken on a mystique all

their own, becoming something they all marveled. No one laughed when she created a solar-powered machine that would feed their dog at regular intervals. As for Gizmo, he stared at the machine that dispensed his food with something like real affection. The old mutt would lie in the sun, one eye closed, the other watching his food bowl hopefully. Becca somehow resisted saying, "But we can do that without a machine." Eunice was discovering the limitless power of the sun, and she was enjoying every new gadget she created.

Even Bethany seemed to be having an easier go of things. She'd always been shy, which was probably why she enjoyed finding work she could do at home—knitting, embroidery, even quilting. Folks had begun placing orders with Bethany for knitted blankets, baby sets and wedding gifts. The pay, if you figured it out per hour, was quite low. Still, she was contributing to the community, and for the time being, that seemed to satisfy her *dat*, though he occasionally dropped a hint about Bethany coming to work at the market.

Becca even found her *dat*'s interference in their social lives endearing. On the Tuesday after the buggy races, he invited yet another widower over for dinner. Becca and her *schweschdern* were unerringly polite, and they'd waited until he'd left before replaying the evening's most awkward moments—laughing until their sides hurt and tears ran down their cheeks. They weren't laughing at the man so much as laughing with him. At least, they hoped Evan Graber was chuckling as he drove home. He had alternately blushed, become tongue-tied and resorted to complimenting the food each time he didn't know what else to say.

Gut *bread*.

This chicken is amazing.

Who knew butter could taste so gut.

Few men, let alone widowers, knew how to respond when finding himself at a table full of women. Becca almost felt sympathy for them, but she knew her *dat* would interpret any such comments as interest, so she kept her feelings on that subject to herself.

It was the following Monday—June 6, to be exact—that Gideon called her over the two-way radio. He hadn't asked for her help on anything in the ten days since their conversation after the buggy races. They'd reviewed his duties at the end of each day, but he had doggedly worked on his own, keeping her at a distance. When she heard the radio crackle, she nearly jumped out of her office chair.

"*Ya.* Becca here."

"We have a situation in the auction house. You might want to come and weigh in."

Becca dropped the paperwork she was sorting and practically jogged over to the auction house.

She spotted Gideon easily enough. Standing on the far side of the large room, several of the auctioneers were watching and waiting.

"What's the problem?"

Gideon pulled off his hat, then nodded toward Jeremy Gingerich, who was their very best auctioneer. Jeremy was thirty-eight, had a booming voice and a likable personality that consistently drew in the crowds. He was also very methodical about his work, always showing up the day before an auction to look through the items that he'd be offering up for sale. The actual auctions were held on Wednesdays, but prospective buyers could preview the items on Tuesday afternoons.

Jeremy was nearly six feet tall, big but not overweight, and dressed in traditional Amish clothes. They'd actually featured him on the market's website before. The brown bushy beard, suspenders, straw hat and twinkle in his eyes raised their clicks to the highest level yet.

"I was looking through the items that Widow King wanted us to auction." He picked up what looked like an old cigar box and handed it to Becca, motioning for her to open it.

Inside were official-looking pieces of paper.

"They're stocks," Gideon confirmed.

They were indeed—for Dell, Microsoft, even Walmart.

"I don't understand."

"Neither do we." James Lapp let out a boisterous laugh, then tried to look serious. It was plain that he was a bit uncertain as to whether he should be laughing or not. James worked in the animal auctions, and he was definitely the youngest in the group.

"Seems to me like someone in Widow King's family was investing in the stock market." Jeremy nodded toward the box that Becca was holding. "Whoever it was picked some real winners."

"You think these are actual stock certificates?"

"Looks like it to me." Jeremy shuffled from one foot to the other. "I definitely don't think she'd want them auctioned."

"Shouldn't these be in a bank deposit box?"

"Yes." Gideon's voice was solid, firm—relaxed, even. When had he become so comfortable around the auction barn workers? "You're going to want to call her."

"No phone." Becca shook her head. "She's packing up, you know. Getting ready to move to Maine and join her *kinner* and *grandkinner.* It's the reason she put so many of her things in the auction."

"In that case, I suppose we should take these to your *dat.*"

It seemed strange to walk from the auction barn to the office with Gideon. They were usually going in different directions, with only a nod or wave at one another. She suspected he was avoiding her after *The Buggy-Race Debacle*—that's how she thought of it now, as if it were the title of an Amish novel.

As they crossed the market grounds, several of the vendors called out greetings to him, and Gideon even waved in response.

"You're acting rather jolly this morning."

"Jolly?"

"At home, relaxed, friendly."

"And that's unusual?" He smiled as he held open the door to the main offices.

"Yes. It's very unusual."

Ten minutes later, they were heading back out of the office and crossing to Nathan's buggy. "I'm a little surprised your *dat* didn't want to do this himself."

"Oh, he's all about encouraging responsibility in his employees."

"Got it."

She didn't add that her *dat* had discussed this with her the previous Sunday. Gideon had met with him after speaking with his parents. He'd explained to her *dat* that he was willing to give the market his full effort, but that he would make a decision after thirty days. Becca's *dat* was hoping that by giving him more responsibility and less oversight, he'd step into the space created for him.

The ride out to Widow King's took fifteen minutes.

The day was so beautiful that Becca found herself relaxing, forgetting about plans and disruptions of plans, where she wanted to be next and what she'd rather be doing. She found herself enjoying the moment.

As they pulled into the drive, Becca realized that Gideon hadn't interrupted her quiet reverie. He was either lost in his own thoughts or enjoying the morning as much as she was. Studying him, she wasn't sure. She was about to ask when Widow King stepped out onto the porch.

"Sarah Yoder, it's *gut* to see you this morning. And you've brought your beau with you." She clapped her hands and smiled. "Come in. Come in. I have some fresh coffee cake that will be just the thing for this fine June morning."

Gideon stepped closer and asked in a low voice, "Sarah? Beau?"

"She has a bit of a memory problem at times."

They followed her inside, passing rows of boxes filled with items that she'd either sell or take with her. Becca stopped and put her hand on top of one that said *Christmas*. She hoped that Elizabeth wasn't giving away her holiday things. That thought was too sad for such a beautiful day.

Soon, they were seated at the kitchen table, and Becca explained who she was and that Gideon worked with her at the auction. "We have something we want you to look at—something that was in your auction items."

Elizabeth King set the coffee cake on a trivet in the middle of the table. It was fresh out of the oven and smelled delicious. Becca's stomach growled appreciatively.

Gideon jumped up to fetch the mugs and hot coffee.

As he filled the mugs and Becca cut the cake, Elizabeth reached for the old box with trembling hands. She was a small woman. It seemed to Becca that she'd been shrinking for years. Nearly ninety years old, she now barely topped five feet. Her *kapp* had slipped back an inch or so, and her hair reminded Becca of the pictures she'd seen of cotton bolls—white and soft and stirring slightly in the breeze that came through the window. Though her summer dress was worn, the fabric looked clean and pressed.

Elizabeth held the box, but she didn't open it. Her eyes had taken on a distant look, as if she were peering into the past.

"This was Burl's special box. He had two that he kept in a drawer on his side of the dresser. Burl would pat them and tell me they would see me through my old age. The other one is packed there with my things. It's full of treasures—rocks, arrowheads, flowers pressed flat between pages of a newspaper. When I open that box, it's as if Burl is sitting beside me. But this box? This box only holds paper." She glanced up at Becca and then Gideon. "How did you come to have it?"

"The box was in your auction items," Gideon said, glancing at Becca as he did.

"You asked my *dat* to auction some of your things," Becca added. "At the market in town."

"Oh, yes. I remember now." She pushed the box back across the table. "I know collectors like old things. Maybe you can get a dollar or two for that cigar box, but I certainly don't need to take it with me to Maine."

"Actually, we think the contents might be valuable." Gideon opened the box and pulled out the top piece of paper.

Viewing it for a second time, Becca agreed with Gideon's assessment that it was the real deal. Words printed on the thick paper indicated the number of shares purchased, the date and the company logo for Dell Computers. There was even a raised seal in one corner.

"These are certificates of stocks," Gideon explained. "They were issued a long time ago, close to thirty years. Do you remember your husband purchasing them?"

"Oh, I don't know." She ran her fingertips over the company logo and gold seal. "Burl always did like to read the *Englisch* newspapers, especially the financial section. He said that we could invest in a company same as we invest in our neighbors. That even though, as Amish, we are called to be set apart, we're also one divine family created by God."

"These are very successful *Englisch* companies," Becca said.

"At least those top few sheets are." Gideon sat back, sipping the coffee and staring at the stack of stocks certificate. "Some of them have gone out of business."

"If they've gone out of business, then they're trash." Elizabeth's brow furrowed in confusion. "Right?"

"Not exactly. People collect old stock certificates now. I think you should allow us to auction the ones from corporations that are no longer functioning."

"And the others?"

"The others you need to take to your banker."

Elizabeth King seemed to think about that a moment. She glanced around the room at the half-packed boxes. Then she sighed. "I don't have time to go to town now. My son is traveling down on a bus. He should be here in a few days. I'm moving to Maine to live with him."

"Yes, we know." Becca felt a sudden urge to comfort

this woman. She couldn't imagine moving away from all you'd ever known at her age. Yes, it sounded fun to Becca. She'd seen the pictures of the harbors and lighthouses and fall colors. But for Elizabeth, she thought it might all be a little frightening. "I know your family will be happy to have you close by."

"He's told me to pack only the necessities."

"That must be hard."

Elizabeth stared down into her coffee, then glanced up and met first Gideon's, then Becca's gaze. "The thing with getting old is you still remember."

"Remember what, exactly?" Gideon pushed away his plate and folded his arms on the table, studying Elizabeth.

"Oh, everything." Elizabeth's smile was bright as she looked around the room, then out the window over the sink.

"I remember all that went before. I remember when we first moved here. I was a young girl then—or it seems that way now." She laughed. "Probably your age, Becca. My life was just beginning, but I didn't know that. I felt old at twenty-two. Imagine that."

"You and Burl had a *gut* life." Becca turned her mug first one way, then the other. "You always seemed to care for one another."

"Oh, *ya*, we did—from the beginning, we did. I catch myself falling into those memories some days. We were young and had no idea all that lay ahead, both the joys and the sorrows. But mostly, now, I remember the joys. I remember laughing and running through the corn, Burl's arms around me, every baby being born. This is where I lived my life, and though I'm moving far away, I won't forget. This old house—it's been a teacher. A friend, even. I suppose that sounds silly."

"Not at all," Gideon said. He cleared his throat.

Becca thought that Gideon looked particularly moved by Elizabeth's musings.

He sat up straighter and asked, "Did you have a banking account in town?"

"Oh, *ya*." Elizabeth named the bank as well as the person who helped her with her accounts.

"How about I take these to him? He may need you to sign some papers, but I suspect he'd be willing to drive out here with them. He can sell the stocks for you and put the money in your account."

When Elizabeth seemed unconvinced, Becca added, "It would no doubt be a help to your family."

The smile returned—if anything, brighter than before. "That would be kind. *Danki*."

"Gem gschehne." Becca and Gideon said the words at the same time, their gazes locking for the briefest of moments.

"We should get back." Gideon stood, carefully pushing the chair in. "Is there anything else you need?"

"Oh, no. I'm doing fine."

Becca cleared the dishes as Gideon walked with Elizabeth out onto the front porch. Becca looked out the window and saw him there, head bent to catch the old woman's words. Gideon Fisher was often overly serious—and a worrywart, if she'd ever met one—but she realized in that moment that he was also kind. He responded well to people, and they to him. Those qualities were important—in a market manager but also in a neighbor or friend.

She understood in that moment that Gideon would

go back to Texas. He'd slip into his old life as easily as Elizabeth was slipping from hers. He'd meet a girl, marry and… What was it Elizabeth had said? He'd have a life filled with joys and sorrows. But mostly joys.

Becca almost envied him that, his future which would follow such a traditional and contented path. Why was it that she couldn't see the same for herself? Why was she always focusing on the next thing? Why was she never quite content?

She didn't share any of those thoughts as they traveled back toward the market. Elizabeth's box sat between them on the buggy seat, right beside Becca's regrets and worries and doubts—feelings that she had absolutely no idea what to do with.

Gideon readied for work on Friday morning, four days after visiting Elizabeth King's home. That particular story had ended well. The stocks were worth more than anyone among the auctioneers had guessed—and they'd all guessed. Elizabeth's son had arrived to accompany her to her new home, and he'd been greeted by a big surprise in the form of a check from Elizabeth's bank. When tears had slipped down the man's face, something inside Gideon had twisted. It wasn't often you saw a man cry, let alone an Amish man. They had been tears of joy, and Gideon had felt a satisfaction unlike anything he'd known before. They had a hand in making this family's life better—he and Jeremy, the other auctioneers, even Becca.

It occurred to him that such a thing was as important as planting and harvesting a crop—perhaps even more important.

"Big to-do at the market this weekend, *ya*?" Nathan

smiled as he shoveled scrambled eggs onto both their plates.

"*Ya*, indeed. Becca says the crowds will be larger than what we had on Memorial Day, and those were quite large."

Nathan filled their mugs and sat down across from Gideon. He had tried telling Nathan that there was no need to fix him breakfast, but the old guy seemed to enjoy sharing the meal together. Gideon had switched his JoJo's pretzel habit to afternoons. He would miss both JoJo's and Nathan when he left.

If he left.

"You're meeting with Amos on Monday."

"I am."

"Any idea what you'll say to him?"

"Honestly—no." Gideon reached for a piece of the fresh bread that Becca's oldest *schweschder* dropped off every week. The Indiana Amish were a different lot, with fancier houses and nicer buggies, but they cared for those in the community same as the families in his hometown of Beeville cared for one another.

He buttered the bread, then added a spoonful of jam, which he meticulously spread out. "Honestly, my mind goes back and forth. Some days, I'm sure that I should head back home. Other days, I realize that I'm enjoying being here."

"Love, respect, priorities."

It had become their mantra, their special code to one another.

"I will pray that you know for certain—in your mind and your heart—what you should do."

"Thanks, Nathan." Gideon finished his breakfast, then stood and carried his dishes to the sink. "I suspect

I might be late coming home. It's bound to be an interesting day."

"Don't worry about me. Melvin is going to pick me up and take me fishing today."

"You two leave some for the *youngies*, okay?"

"*Ya*, we will, for sure and certain."

Gideon arrived at the market thirty minutes before his regular time, and still the place was abuzz with activity. The June Weekend Flea Market didn't actually begin until noon, but additional vendors were there early, setting up tables filled with goods they hoped to sell.

Several of his regular vendors called out a greeting as he made his way across the market grounds. Amos wasn't in his office, but Becca was in theirs. She wore a peach-colored dress and a freshly starched white apron and *kapp*. Often she drove him to distraction with her energy and optimism and endless certainty, but like Nathan, the vendors and the entire market, he would miss her.

His feelings for her were complicated. Some days, she seemed like a pesky younger *schweschder*. Other days—well, other days he thought he'd been out in the heat too long, because she looked like someone he would ask out to dinner. He didn't. He wasn't a fool. Becca Fisher was not in the market for a beau, unless he happened to be driving a bus headed out of town.

She'd been giving him *space*—her words, not his. He suspected she was still embarrassed about the buggy-day setup that had gone awry. At the moment, she was trying to juggle a large box of water bottles, a stack of flyers and cardboard hand fans. The fans and water bottles sported their market logo and the web page address.

"Let me take that."

"They're not heavy, just awkward." She surrendered the large box of water bottles and snatched up the camera from her desk, looping the strap around her neck.

"Still can't believe your bishop allows pictures."

"Tasteful pictures, Gideon."

"Ah, well, if they're tasteful…" Actually, Becca's photography habit had stopped bothering him several weeks ago. It wasn't like she was tweeting the pictures or posting them on Instagram or Snapchat. Honestly, Gideon didn't understand what any of those things were, but he did understand the value of good promotional material. Becca was a natural at promoting her father's market. He wondered if she'd do the same for MDS missions. That thought caused his stomach to clench, so he pushed it from his mind.

Together they carried everything outside into another day of bright sunshine.

He was always surprised when the sun didn't hit him with the ferocity of a Texas summer day. Instead, there was a gentle breeze from the north. The temperature was supposed to rise to eighty-eight degrees—a real scorcher, by Indiana standards. It felt like spring to Gideon.

"These must have been delivered after we left, or you'd already have them at the gate."

"Would you believe the delivery receipt says they came at seven last night? Who works until seven in the evening?"

"An Amish farmer harvesting his crop."

"Sometimes."

"A doctor."

"I suppose."

"An *Englisch* delivery driver."

"I guess I deserve your ridiculous answers. I did ask

you to answer that question, though now I'm rather regretting it."

He bumped his shoulder against hers, causing laughter to spill from her lips. Becca had very kissable lips, if there was such a thing. Not that Gideon knew from having tried. He couldn't see himself doing that.

"Ready for the weekend?"

"I am."

She didn't ask if he'd made his decision, and he appreciated that. She'd managed to stay out of his business. He knew that wasn't her nature. Which was probably why he started kidding her.

"It's killing you. Isn't it?"

"What?"

"Not knowing what I'm going to do."

"Oh, that."

"Yes, that."

"You'd tell me if you wanted me to know."

"I'd tell you if I knew." And then they were at the gate, and work precluded any other conversation. She placed the water bottles on the counter of the welcome booth, where young Ada had been drafted into working.

"Why do I have to stay in this booth all day, Becca?"

"Because you lost your job at Yoder's."

"For sitting in a rocking chair. Since when is that a crime?"

"Since they were paying you to stock shelves."

"Everyone needs a rest now and then."

"The rocking chairs are for customers."

"I had an entire group around me, asking questions about Amish life. What was I supposed to do? Leave them and go restock garden tools?"

Gideon tried to act as if he wasn't listening in on their

conversation, but then he started laughing, which caused Ada to laugh. She always had a bright attitude, even when she was being corralled into another job. Becca tried to give them both a disappointed look as she unpacked hand fans and stacked them on the right-hand side of where Ada was supposed to stand.

"Water bottles on the left. Fans on the right. Maps in your hand. Do you remember what we went over last night?"

"Smile at the customers."

"Always."

"Make sure they have a map."

"It has our web page. Hopefully, they'll take it home with them and click on our site and buy something."

"Then I offer them a water bottle or a fan."

"*Gut* girl."

"What if they don't want a water bottle or fan? What if I get overrun with *Englischers*? What if I need a bathroom break?"

"Bethany promised to be here by ten. She'll cover the booth during your breaks and lunch."

"She'll probably bring her knitting and ignore everyone. I should have thought of that."

"You don't knit."

"I could learn."

Gideon unpacked as many of the water bottles as would fit on the counter, then he stored the still half-full box on the ground inside the booth. He rather enjoyed the banter between Becca and Ada. It made him feel like he was part of their family. It made him miss home a little less.

"Both of you stay right there." Becca hustled out of

the booth. Stepping back about ten feet, she lifted her camera and said, "On three."

Gideon glanced at Ada, and they both started laughing. On three, he ducked his head, and she turned to the side.

"Perfect!" Becca practically squealed. "You two are very *gut* at this."

She showed them the picture on the camera's playback screen. As he suspected, it could have been a picture of any Amish guy and girl—which was what they wanted. Give the customers a feel of the plain and simple life, but without either of them attempting to be a model. Basically, they saw the straw hat of an Amish guy looking down at the welcome flyers and an Amish girl in profile.

"We look *gut* together, Gideon. Maybe we should go to work for an Amish magazine. Are there Amish magazines?" Ada was leaning against the counter of the booth. "Anything would be better than being the welcome gal."

Gideon tossed her a sympathetic smile. "You know, Ada…you could take over my job."

"Would I be Becca's boss?"

Becca looked up from the camera. "I'd be gone, *schweschder*. That's the point of finding a replacement."

"I'm not interested, then. It would only be fun if I was able to boss you around. Honestly, I don't think I'd be very *gut* at your job, Becca. Besides, you two are a *wunderbaar* team. *Dat* said so last night."

Gideon turned an inquisitive look toward Becca, but her eyebrows shot up in mock surprise. "No idea what she's talking about."

The way that she blushed made Gideon think that might not be true. Was she embarrassed? Why?

As Becca and Gideon walked away, Ada called out, "Don't just leave me here."

"Try to enjoy the morning. Bethany will be here before you know it."

Becca was walking backward and nearly ran into a woman pulling a wagon full of birdhouses that she hoped to sell. Gideon reached out for Becca's arm, pulling her out of the woman's path.

"That's an hour and a half away." When Becca only waved at her, Ada called out in an even louder voice, "Time is supposed to hop when you're having fun, but I don't think it will."

That caused them both to laugh. Another Ada-ism.

He would miss those too. And suddenly, a thought nearly knocked him off his feet. He would like to see Christmas in Indiana. The extravaganza and gingerbread competition and yard decorations. Maybe—just possibly—Texas wasn't all he'd built it up to be. Maybe happiness wasn't where you were but who you were with. Maybe he'd been looking at his future all wrong.

Chapter Eight

Gideon awoke the next morning with the same bone weariness he associated with working in the fields all day. The market had closed at eight the night before. He and Becca had stayed until half past nine helping vendors close and preparing for the next day.

Fortunately, the market was only open half a day on Saturday—from eight until two. They had church the next day, and on Monday, he'd tell Amos his decision. He planned to work through the next week, which would take him exactly to the one-month mark. He realized as he dressed that his mind seemed to have already made a decision without consulting his emotions. Perhaps that was as it should be.

For breakfast, Nathan made French toast topped with locally made syrup. It really hit the spot. At this rate, Nathan's cooking would surpass JoJo's and his kitchen would become Gideon's new favorite place. Though he had to admit, he'd grown rather fond of his daily pretzel. He'd miss those when he returned to Beeville. His mind flashed back on the thoughts he'd had the night before—thoughts of spending Christmas with Becca.

He didn't linger there, though. As was his usual method of dealing with all things uncomfortable, he pushed the thoughts away and focused on work.

The morning progressed in much the same manner as the day before. He helped Becca take more supplies to the welcome booth. Ada was once again ensconced there, though she'd found a stool to perch on rather than stand all day.

"*Dat* had to really pull my arm to get me to come back today."

"Do you mean *twist* your arm?" Becca smiled at Ada.

"I mean *pull*. In fact, he had to practically pull me into the buggy. I wasn't too eager to get up. The excellent news is that he promised I could have next week off to look for gainful employment. Can you believe that's what he calls it? The only thing I seem to gain from working is a headache."

"You're a peach, sis."

"Do you think so?"

"I do." Becca handed her a bottle filled with ice water. Gideon remembered her once saying that Ada was the family pet. It was plain how much they all adored her, and somehow it didn't make her haughty or spoiled. Ada was like the runt of the litter—the one everyone pulled for and encouraged.

Gideon winked at her, but resisted the urge to reach out and tug on her *kapp* strings. "Call if you need anything, Ada."

"I don't have a phone."

"Just tell someone. They'll find me."

Becca was grinning at him as they walked back across the market square. Their plan was for him to cover the west side of the market, which included the Backyard

Barnyard and the red parking area. Becca would cover the east side and the blue parking area. At eleven, they would switch sides.

"I worry when you smile like that. Are you a cat? Are you hiding a canary in your mouth?" He acted as if he was going to pry open her mouth, and she ducked away.

"No canary. I was thinking about how much you've changed in the last month."

"I have not."

"Oh, yes you have. You never smiled when you first came here."

"I didn't?"

"You were quite serious."

"I'm still serious." He tried to school his expression into something more somber, but he couldn't hold it. He couldn't look at Becca and not smile. When had that happened?

"You acted as if you were afraid to get to know anyone."

"This place definitely takes some getting used to." He no longer felt lost or overwhelmed walking through the market grounds. In fact, it felt as if he knew this place as well as he knew the family farm back home.

They parted ways with a high five, something else he had rarely done before a month ago. The morning passed quickly. He was considering taking a lunch break when a familiar face appeared in the crowd. He almost thought he was hallucinating, but there was no doubt that the man walking his way was David Hershberger.

"If it isn't Gideon Fisher. I thought that was your ugly mug I saw." The two old friends embraced. Actually, Gideon hadn't spent that much time with David the last few years. He'd rarely left the farm unless it was for church services. But when they were *youngies* fresh out of the schoolroom, they'd often seen each other.

"David. What…what are you doing here?"

"Visiting family. Didn't I tell you I was coming?"

"*Nein*. So, you came up on the bus?"

"I did. Long ways from Beeville, isn't it?" David held out his arms. "Just look at all the people. More than we see at home in a year."

"Indeed. Say, I was about to break for lunch. Want to join me?"

Gideon had forgotten all about the fact that he was supposed to meet Becca. No matter—she found him. Becca seemed to have an innate sense of where everyone was at any given time. As she called his name and walked toward him, Gideon saw her as David must have—young, pretty, vibrant.

"Who's the gal?"

Fortunately, Becca pushed quickly through the crowd to stand beside them, so Gideon was able to avoid the suggestive arc of David's eyebrows.

"Becca, this is my friend from Beeville, David Hershberger."

"*Gut* to meet you. Did you come all the way from Texas for today's flea market?"

"I did not. I came to see my cousins, who actually live over in Goshen. They were all coming to the flea market today, so I thought I'd come along and look for this guy." He playfully pushed Gideon, causing him to brush up against Becca.

She blushed slightly, and David gave him another inquiring look.

Gideon took a discreet step away from Becca. "I

FREE BOOKS GIVEAWAY

2 FREE **ROMANCE** BOOKS!

2 FREE **SUSPENSE** BOOKS!

GET UP TO FOUR FREE BOOKS & TWO FREE GIFTS WORTH OVER $20!

We pay for everything!

See Details Inside

YOU pick your books –
WE pay for everything.
You get up to FOUR New Books an
TWO Mystery Gifts...absolutely FRE

Dear Reader,

I am writing to announce the launch of a huge **FREE BOOI GIVEAWAY**... and to let you know that YOU are entitled to choose up to FOUR fantastic books that WE pay for.

Try **Love Inspired® Romance Larger-Print** books and fall in love with inspirational romances that take you on an uplifting journey of faith, forgiveness and hope.

Try **Love Inspired® Suspense Larger-Print** books where courage and optimism unite in stories of faith and love in the face of danger.

Or TRY BOTH!

In return, we ask just one favor: Would you please participate in our brief Reader Survey? We'd love to hear from you.

This FREE BOOKS GIVEAWAY means that your introductory shipment is completely free, <u>even the shipping</u>! If you decide to continue, you can look forward to curated month shipments of brand-new books from your selected series, always at a discount off the cover price! <u>Plus you can canc any time</u>. Who could pass up a deal like that?

Sincerely

Pam Powers

Pam Powers
For Harlequin Reader Servic

Complete the survey below and return it today to receive up to 4 FREE BOOKS and FREE GIFTS guaranteed!

FREE BOOKS GIVEAWAY
Reader Survey

1
Do you prefer books which reflect Christian values?

○ YES   ○ NO

2
Do you share your favorite books with friends?

○ YES   ○ NO

3
Do you often choose to read instead of watching TV?

○ YES   ○ NO

YES! Please send me my Free Rewards, consisting of **2 Free Books from each series I select** and Free Mystery Gifts. I understand that I am under no obligation to buy anything, no purchase necessary see terms and conditions for details.

☐ **Love Inspired® Romance Larger-Print** (122/322 IDL GRSJ)
☐ **Love Inspired® Suspense Larger-Print** (107/307 IDL GRSJ)
☐ **Try Both** (122/322 & 107/307 IDL GRSU)

FIRST NAME	LAST NAME

ADDRESS

APT.#	CITY

STATE/PROV.	ZIP/POSTAL CODE

EMAIL ☐ Please check this box if you would like to receive newsletters and promotional emails from Harlequin Enterprises ULC and its affiliates. You can unsubscribe anytime.

LI/LIS-122-FBG22

thought I'd take David over to JoJo's for lunch. Care to join us?"

"Can't. I grabbed a granola bar earlier."

"Do you need me to stay?"

"Not at all. East side's looking all in order. Take as long as you'd like, just be sure to be back in time to help with closing at two."

Gideon glanced at his watch. It was only a few minutes after eleven, but his stomach was growling. "Sounds *gut*. Want me to bring back a pretzel for you?"

"*Nein.* But *danki*."

And then she was gone, ducking back through the crowd.

David let out a long whistle. "You're going to have to tell me all about that one."

On the walk down to JoJo's, Gideon gave a succinct description of his time at the market, his growing friendship with Becca and her family, and the big decision he needed to make in the next few days.

David waited until they were sitting down with fresh pretzels and cold lemonade to confront his friend. "Are you *narrisch*? Why would you leave this to go back to nowhere Texas?"

"I love nowhere Texas."

"Uh-huh, we all do." David dipped his cinnamon-sugar pretzel into the homemade icing. He'd always had a sweet tooth, and he groaned with the first bite. "These are amazing."

"Right?"

They ate for a few minutes before David picked up the conversation again. "It seems to me that you're forgetting how lonely it is, how the work causes one day to bleed into another, how you can go months without meeting someone new."

"I guess, but those things never bothered me before."

"Sometimes they don't until you see how the other side lives."

Gideon dipped the last bite of his Parmesan pretzel into the remaining cheddar cheese, buying himself time to answer. "I know what you're saying is true, but it's not all roses here. There are a lot of people. The Indiana Amish are quite different from our community, and if I take the job permanently, I'd be committing to staying here for years."

"But that's not what you said."

"What's not what I said?"

"You said that you have to tell Becca's *dat* whether you'll work through the ninety-day period."

"Okay."

"That's not saying you'll be here for years. Only until the end of summer. If someone invited me to be anywhere other than South Texas in July and August, I'd take them up on it in a heartbeat." He sighed and looked around, as if he was catching a glimpse at paradise. "My family isn't as big as yours, as you know. Only me and one *bruder* to help *Dat* with the crops. It was hard for me to get away for a week."

Gideon slumped back in his chair and finished the lemonade. It was sweet and tart and cold. In other words—perfect. Finally, he said, "You're right that I was thinking of it as a full commitment. But what's the point in putting off the decision? Should I decide to stay until the end of summer, I'm going to be right back where I am at this moment, only it'll be sixty days from now."

"A lot can happen in sixty days."

"Like what?"

"You could find hidden talents and decide you love the job."

Gideon rolled his eyes.

"Seriously. You could realize that you're a *gut* fit for market manager. You always were the organized one."

"I guess." He didn't want to admit that he liked that part of running the market, because doing so would suggest that perhaps he'd been wrong about his lifework. He was a farmer. Wasn't he? Then again, he had grown to like the people he worked with at the market. He'd come to think of all the vendors as parts of a clock—as long as they all worked together, then the market ran smoothly.

"And…" His friend grinned and waited until he had Gideon's full attention. "You could fall in love with Becca."

Gideon laughed off that remark, then stood and cleared their table, avoiding any eye contact with his old friend.

Why had David said such a thing?

You could fall in love with Becca.

Why had he even put that thought in his mind? Now it was stuck there, playing over and over in a loop.

As they walked back toward the market, David filled him in on happenings in Beeville. They'd had a single rain that had washed out the main road into their community. "Only lasted for five hours, but you would have thought it was the days of Noah."

"I'm sure the rain was welcome."

"Indeed. So tell me about where you're living while you're here. With Becca's family?"

"Nein." He told David about Nathan, how he liked to cook and play horseshoes and make walking sticks.

"I sort of think of him as an *onkel*. He's full of life and energy in spite of his age."

"And you have your own room?"

"Ya."

"That must be nice. Since I've known you, you've always shared a room with at least two *bruders*."

As they were about to part ways at the market entrance, David shook his hand. "I spoke with your parents before I left. They're proud of you—proud that you're trying something new and different. They asked me to tell you that they all miss you, and they'll either see you at the end of summer or at Christmas."

Gideon nodded and embraced his friend.

End of summer or Christmas...

A gut *fit for market manager...*

You could fall in love with Becca.

His friend's words were planted firmly in Gideon's mind. Perhaps he had been thinking about this all wrong. It wasn't as if he'd never see his family again if he decided to stay. Of course he would still visit over the holidays and on special occasions. The bus trip was a long one, but he hadn't minded it so much. It had been interesting to watch the country roll by outside the bus's window.

And he knew, in his heart, that he was a *gut* fit for market manager—or rather, assistant market manager. Like farming, he'd found his rhythm. The day-to-day tasks and responsibilities no longer seemed overwhelming. As he tossed and turned in his bed that night, he realized that he was very blessed to be able to be good at more than one job. He had a choice. How many people could say that?

Farmer?

Or manager?

He flopped onto his back and tried to envision a life spent working on a farm and then compare it to a life spent managing the market. He'd never really considered the latter. He'd come only because his parents had insisted. Could it be that they were right?

Love. Respect. Priorities.

He would be showing them respect by fulfilling his original promise to stay ninety days.

Their bishop back home was fond of saying that *Gotte* had a purpose and a plan for every life. Gideon was pretty sure the sentiment was found in the Old Testament, but he couldn't remember where. He supposed the exact verse wasn't as important as the intent of the words.

Did *Gotte* have a purpose and plan for his life?

Was that purpose, that plan, for him to stay in Shipshewana, Indiana?

But as he yawned and drifted off into a much-needed sleep, it wasn't those things that followed him into his dreams. It was David saying that he might fall in love with Becca. And Ada saying that they made a *gut* team. And Becca smiling up at him as she bumped shoulders, then laughed at something he'd said.

He woke the next morning certain of what he was going to do.

Though he had no idea if it would work out for the better or if it would, in the end, break his heart. He would be stepping out in faith, and that was something that Gideon Fisher had never done before.

Becca knew that Gideon was up to something from the first moment she saw him in their church service. He was smiling broadly—regardless of what she'd said the day before, which was still a bit unusual. He was also avoiding her. She was sure of it. He hadn't looked her way even once. Ada bumped against her as she tried to squeeze onto the row where all the Yoder *schweschdern* were sitting. For some reason, they always sat oldest to youngest—Sarah, Becca, Eunice, Bethany and Ada.

If she reached far back in her mind, she could remember her *mamm* sitting on the far side of Sarah, holding baby Ada in her arms. Becca had only been seven at the time of her mother's death, but she retained quite vivid memories of her. She could still see her *mamm* smiling down the row of girls. Perhaps that was why they still sat that way. Ada probably couldn't remember their *mamm*, though she loved to listen to the stories of things their *mamm* had done and said. She had only been one year old when their *mamm* died of uterine cancer. They'd barely known she was sick, and then suddenly, one cold winter's night, she was simply gone.

The ache that Becca had felt for so many years had since vanished. She still missed her *mamm*, but she'd grown accustomed to life without her. Was that the way with loss? Did the body and the heart learn to go on because there was no alternative? Or did the heart go on as a sort of tribute to the person who had passed?

She found herself lost in those kinds of thoughts when Eunice nudged her, and they stood for the final hymn. Becca didn't even remember the sermon. As they sang "I Have Decided," she thought she could pick out Gideon's voice from across the aisle and two rows back. He stood between her *dat* and Nathan. He had a baritone voice. Why was that surprising? Someone serious and tall should have a baritone voice. That didn't explain the way goose bumps ran down her arms when she focused on his singing. And then, of course, once she had singled out his voice, she couldn't not hear it.

While they were helping in the serving line, Sarah leaned closer and asked, "Do you think today's the day?"

"What day?"

"The day Gideon announces his decision."

"Maybe. I don't know. Before the end of this week. In fact, I wouldn't be surprised if he's already bought his bus ticket home." She pushed the platter of cold chicken toward the front of the table and pulled back the nearly empty plate of sliced ham. "I suppose I can't blame him, but why can't things work out for me, just once?"

Sarah leaned closer, their *kapps* nearly brushing. "If that's your wish, it just might be coming true." Then she put her arm around Becca and gave her shoulders a squeeze before moving down the table to help one of the Schwartz twins fill their plates.

What did that mean?

Becca glanced after Sarah, then looked in the direction of her *dat*. What she saw then nearly caused her to drop the plate of deviled eggs she was holding. Her *dat* was clapping Gideon on the back and laughing. Gideon stared at his shoes, then looked at her *dat* and finally glanced over at her.

Becca immediately stared down at the plates of food and began shuffling them haphazardly.

"Better slow down there, or you're going to make someone dizzy." Eunice had seen what Becca had seen, though, because she stepped closer and murmured, "Looks to me like your beau is staying."

"He's not—" But before she could finish the sentence,

Eunice rushed away to carry ninety-five-year-old Olivia Miller's plate.

Becca stayed at the serving line as long as possible. Finally, she filled her own plate and walked over to where her friends were sitting—the same friends she'd tried to set up with Gideon. Janet and Hannah made room for her to sit in the middle. Fortunately, no one spoke of her ill-fated matchmaking. The *gut* thing about the group of girls she hung out with was that no one held a grudge. They were quick to move on to new things— and this week, that new thing was Olivia Miller's great-grandson, who had come from Ohio to visit.

"He's dreamy," Emily confessed. "All that blond hair."

Claire leaned in as if to share a secret. "He was over at Howie's when we went there last week. He seemed very sociable. My *bruder* invited him to the singing to-night, and he said he'd try to come."

Which started all four of her friends giggling and talking about the evening's youth event. Becca hadn't been to one of those in years, and she was surprised to hear they still went. Wasn't twenty-four a bit old for such things? But then, the four girls she was sitting with were all a few years younger. All of Becca's friends who were her age or older were married and sitting with their husbands and babies.

"Something wrong with your potato salad, Becca?" Janet cocked her head. "We can ask someone at the end of the table to fetch you something different."

"*Nein*. It's fine. I'm just not hungry." That last sentence was something she'd rarely uttered. Becca had always enjoyed a healthy appetite.

Her friends suddenly fell silent, but it wasn't until they

darted glances over her head that she realized someone was standing behind her.

She didn't need to turn around to see who it was.

Hannah cleared her throat. "Hi, Gideon."

"Care to sit with us?" Janet asked. "We can scooch in."

"No problem at all," Emily assured him.

"Actually, I was wanting to talk to Becca."

Becca somehow managed to swallow the forkful of ham she'd stuffed in her mouth. "Me?" It came out garbled. As her friends giggled, she grabbed her glass of water, downed half of it and then craned her head back, which meant she was looking at Gideon upside down. Was he smiling or frowning, serious or laughing? Hard to tell from that angle.

"Obviously, you're still eating. Sorry. I can come back."

"*Nein.* Now is fine." Extracting herself from the crowded bench of the picnic table wasn't easy. When she nearly tripped and Gideon caught her arm, Becca noticed the girls sending each other looks. Great. Now they'd think there was something going on between them. There was definitely *nothing* going on between them. He'd barely glanced her way all morning.

He waited while she gathered up her plate and glass, deposited them in their respective receptacles and then wiped off her hands.

"Maybe we could take a walk over by the goat pen."

Gideon couldn't have known how much she loved goats. She did. She loved the way they ran about, the way they'd climb on top of anything and the softness of their ears. Plus, there were quite a few of them at the

Mast farm. Benjamin had been raising goats for years. He had several breeds and quite a few play areas.

"Didn't realize that Samuel's *dat* raises goats."

"Oh, *ya*. He sells the milk—some to individuals and some to the cheese factory down the road."

They both stopped and watched a large brown goat with white ears walk across a log. There were several items in the pen for the goats to climb on, including a stack of carefully placed milk crates and a pile of old tires. Becca knew that Benjamin Mast occasionally ran an ad in the local paper saying he'd dispose of any tires *Englischers* had lying around for free. He disposed of them here, in his field. The *Englischers* were free of some trash, and the goats had a new structure to climb on. It was a win-win situation.

Gideon crossed his arms over the top of the fence. "I know next to nothing about goats. What kind are these?"

"Nubian. Samuel's father, Ben—he'll talk your ear off if you ask him about them, so prepare yourself. He's tried several kinds over the years, but he claims that Nubians are popular because they're less trouble and their milk has five percent butterfat."

"I can't believe you remember that."

"Ada tried to talk *Dat* into buying some a few years back. She had this entire presentation to show him, but when he told her the goats would be her responsibility and she'd have to tend to them before and after school…"

"She changed her mind."

"Yup. Said she wasn't ready to light the candle at both ends."

Gideon started laughing. "Sounds like something Ada would say. Why do you suppose she gets every saying wrong?"

"It's not because she's stupid. Ada's smart as they come, but her mind works differently." Becca positively could not handle this attempt at casual conversation any longer. She turned away from the goats, stuck her hands into her apron pockets and leveled her most serious look at Gideon. "I know you didn't want to talk to me about goats or my *schweschder.*"

"True."

"Out with it."

"I spoke to your *dat* earlier and let him know my decision."

Becca didn't think it mattered to her. Or rather, she told herself that she was prepared for the worst. "I saw. I can't imagine why he was laughing when you told him you're leaving, but I saw you two speaking."

"I'm not leaving."

"What?"

"I told him I'm happy to stay for the agreed-upon ninety days."

"Huh."

"Huh?"

"What do you want me to say?"

Gideon took off his hat, slapped it against his pants leg and placed it back on his head. Finally, he admitted, "I thought you'd be happy."

"Well, I am. Of course I am. But I'm surprised."

"You look irritated. I'm quite familiar with that expression."

"Give me a minute to get used to the idea. I thought you'd pretty much made up your mind in the other direction."

"*Ya.* Me too."

They walked along the fence line until they found a

bench that had been placed in the shade of a maple tree. It was a perfect spot for a sunny June day. She didn't want to sit on that bench with Gideon Fisher. In every romance story she'd ever read—and there'd been a fair amount of them during her teens—the man and woman shared a romantic moment on a bench under a tree.

Gideon sat on the bench.

Reluctantly, Becca joined him, careful to keep a large space between them. Her *dat* was probably watching. No need to start his train of thought chugging off in that direction.

They watched the goats in the adjacent field, laughed at the children playing a game of tag, even studied the clouds rolling in from the west.

"Are you used to the idea yet?"

She glanced his direction to see if he was teasing her, but all she saw was curiosity and maybe…concern.

"*Ya.* For sure and certain, it's going to be nice to have your help around the market for sixty more days."

"Ah. So that's the sticky part—isn't it?" When she only nodded, he added, "I said the same thing to David."

"David?"

"My friend from Beeville."

"Is that why you changed your mind?"

"Maybe." He reached down and broke off a blade of tall grass, studied it and then popped it in the side of his mouth. "Sometimes, when a thing becomes stuck in your head, it helps to hear another person's perspective."

"David unstuck the thing in your head?"

"He helped me see your community from an outsider's point of view. I wouldn't be surprised if he moves here. He plainly loves it."

"Any chance he'd take our job?"

Gideon laughed. "Don't be giving that away yet."

"But that's the thing, see." She turned to him now and waited for his gaze to meet hers. "If it's just putting off the inevitable, then what's the point?"

He reached out and brushed her *kapp* string behind her shoulder. The look he gave her sent a wave of delightful shivers down her arm, so she turned to study the children rather than stare into his blue eyes. The last thing she needed to do was develop a crush on Gideon Fisher.

"I said practically those exact words to David." He cleared his throat. "I think it's time for me to give this place a real try. The first few weeks I was here, I was upset because my parents insisted that I come. It was sort of like...well, it was like being pushed out of the nest, which was a pretty uncomfortable feeling."

"I'm sure it was."

"David helped me see that it's not as if I'm being banished from Beeville. My hometown—it's still there."

"So?"

"So maybe I need to stop worrying about not being in Beeville at this very moment. It hasn't disappeared from the planet. It will always be there if I need it, as will my family."

"Sounds like an awfully mature attitude."

"Maybe it's time that I give *here* a chance." He stood, tossed away the piece of grass and then did something very strange. He held out his hand to her.

Becca stared at it; then, realizing he was only offering to help her up, she placed her hand in his. He didn't let go, though. He laced his fingers with hers and said, "How about you and I go and have a look at that dessert table?"

Which was how she found herself walking back toward their group, holding hands with Gideon Fisher and wondering what turn her life had just taken and what she was going to do about it. Because there wasn't a single scenario where she could see this ending well. Though a part of her—a rather large part of her—still wanted to give it a try.

Chapter Nine

The next two weeks passed in a blur. The market, if anything, was busier than in previous years. The fact that Becca split the assistant-manager duties evenly with Gideon meant that she had a few hours' time on her hands—something she wasn't used to at all. It also meant that she didn't see him much.

If he was handling the auction barns, she was with the vendors.

If he took the blue parking area, she took the red.

As early June slipped toward the middle of summer, it seemed that wherever she was working, Gideon was working on the opposite side of the market.

Becca told herself that was how things should be.

There was no way she missed someone that she'd known such a short amount of time and had held hands with once.

She needed to put that memory out of her mind.

What was the point in dwelling on it? The thought that they might have a romantic relationship was foolish. Plainly, he had arrived at the same conclusion, as he'd barely spoken to her since that Sunday. Either she'd be leaving Shipshewana or he would be. What would be the point in starting a relationship now?

At least, that was what she told herself as she tossed and turned at night.

The summer days were longer, and she fell into the habit of taking meandering walks around their farm—through the garden, which was flourishing; past the hayfields, and around the pond. She was restless, and the walks helped. She'd never been a particularly moody person, but she found herself alternately flushed with irritation or tearing up because she felt tender toward people, places, even animals.

What was wrong with her?

Why was she so out of sorts?

It was late on Thursday afternoon when she looked up and saw Gideon walking across the field toward her. Her first thought was that something was wrong at the market, but he didn't look upset. Plus, the market was operating more smoothly than ever. That was why she'd begun taking off at three in the afternoon.

She stayed where she was, leaning against a tree; one eye on the pond, the other on Gideon. When he raised a hand in greeting, she did the same. And then he was there, standing in front of her, looking all tall and handsome and content. When had he become so content?

She pushed down the irritation that was becoming so familiar and plastered on what she hoped was a friendly smile. Unfortunately, he didn't fall for it.

"Still put out with me, I see."

Instead of denying it, she crossed her arms and waited for him to explain why he was there.

"Haven't seen you around the market much."

"You're doing such a great job, I barely need to be there."

"That's a *gut* thing, right?"

"Yeah, Gideon. That's a *gut* thing." She sighed heavily, then turned back toward the pond.

"Any fish in there?"

"Of course there's fish."

"Can you eat them?"

Becca tried to hold on to her irritation but failed miserably. Instead of answering him, she flopped on the ground, pulled her knees up and encircled them with her arms, then rested her head on top. She stared at the pond, thinking of how she had spent every day of her life on this property. So why wasn't she more excited about the possibility of leaving?

Gideon sat beside her. "Whatcha thinking about?"

She felt hyperaware of everything about him—his clean scent, the way that his hair flopped over his collar and, of course, those blue eyes that seemed to always take in everything.

"How we used to beg *Dat* to bring us back here to fish. He would, too. Even *Mamm* would come and make a picnic of it. All we ever caught was sunfish, which of course we'd throw back in. But in my mind, those fish rivaled Jonah's whale."

"How old were you when your *mamm* passed?"

"Seven. Seems like forever ago in some ways. But in other ways, it feels like yesterday."

"You still miss her."

"Of course."

"Tell me about her."

Becca cocked her head, but she didn't look at him. She looked out over the farm. It almost felt like if she tried hard enough, she could see into the past. "Sarah looks the most like her, I think. *Mamm* was handy with fixing things around the house. That's probably where Eunice's mechanical talents come from."

"What about Bethany and Ada?"

"They were both very young when she passed— Bethany was only two, and Ada was an infant. We have some of the things that *Mamm* made, though—knitted, crocheted, even embroidered. I like to think that Bethany inherited her talent from *Mamm*."

"And Ada? Did she get her Ada-isms from your *mamm*?"

"Not that, but I remember that her attitude was pleasant. Don't get me wrong—she wasn't a saint. One Sunday, Sarah and I decided to go frog hunting in our Sunday dresses—*Mamm* was not pleased. She made us wash our own clothes the next day. Mind you, I was only six, but I never hunted for frogs in my Sunday clothes again."

Gideon must have glimpsed something melancholy in her expression because he said, "I didn't mean to make you sad."

She shook her head. "I still miss her, but I'm not sad. I only wish that I could hug her one more time."

He apparently didn't know what to say to that, so he waited.

The tune for "O Come All Ye Faithful" popped into her head. She didn't realize she was humming it until Gideon gave her a look, and then they both laughed at the same time.

"Maybe you inherited your love for Christmas from your *mamm*."

Becca sat up straighter. "You could be right. I remember stringing popcorn and berries and wrapping it around the porch railing with her. And baking cookies. And sitting next to her as *Dat* read the Christmas story."

He let that memory settle between them, and even his silence seemed like a tangible thing. Finally, he smiled and said, "One mystery explained—the mystery of Becca's Christmas fascination."

He pulled up a handful of weeds, tossed them in the air and smiled like he'd done something noteworthy. She caught herself staring at his hands, remembering what they felt like holding hers. She shook her head, attempting to clear it, then gave up and pressed her palms against her cheeks.

"Am I giving you a headache?"

"You are."

"Should I go?" His voice had dropped an octave. "I will, if you want me to. It's just that…"

"What?"

"I've missed you, Becca."

"You see me every day at the market."

"From a distance. If I walk in a room, you rush off. We never eat lunch together anymore or go for a pretzel."

"Still have that pretzel habit going on, do you?"

He patted his stomach, ducked his head and smiled shyly. "Actually, I don't know if it was a pretzel habit or a Becca habit."

When she didn't answer, he reached for her hand. "Have I offended you in some way?"

"Nein." Her voice was barely a whisper.

"What then?"

"Six weeks. You have six weeks left here if you don't accept the job, and I have six weeks left here if you stay."

"And?"

"And what's the point in pursuing anything?"

"So, you *do* want to date me."

"Ugh. You are so arrogant."

"No, I'm not. You know I'm not. I'm hopeful."

Becca pulled her hand away, hopped up and brushed off the back of her dress. "You're different. I don't know what's happened to you. Where's the Gideon who was so moody and discontented?"

Instead of being upset by her words, Gideon laughed. "I'd heard women were hard to please."

"What is that supposed to mean?" Now she stood facing him, hands on her hips, the irritation once again flaring; but then it quickly disappeared and was replaced by something else—something that began in her stomach and worked its way up to her cheeks. He was too adorable, standing there holding his hat in his hands and smiling at her awkwardly.

Gideon cleared his throat. "It means I have no experience with this. I didn't date much as a *youngie*."

"Seriously?"

They'd begun walking back toward the house. All the frustration that had been pent-up inside Becca seemed to melt away. She became aware of a warmth inside, and she almost laughed at the image in her mind of the sun sending out its strong rays across the fields, across her.

"Sure. *Ya.* I was shy as a boy."

"Hard to imagine."

"And then, when I was out of school, I suppose I hid away on the farm. I didn't think of it that way. There was always plenty of work to do, and I enjoyed having a task that I knew how to complete. By the time I realized that the farm might not be enough, I looked around and everyone was paired up."

"Back up. Did you just say the farm wasn't enough?

Your Texas farm? The same one you have been longing for since the day you stepped off the bus?"

He laughed again and bumped his shoulder against hers. She loved it when they were like this—completely comfortable with one another. This was what she'd been missing.

"You took me by surprise when you said you were staying—and then, holding my hand at church, well, that was a surprise too."

"You didn't seem to mind."

"I didn't!" She exhaled slowly, once again fighting to control her emotions. She needed to be honest with Gideon. This was her chance. Besides, she was tired of keeping everything pent-up.

"You've messed up my life, Gideon. I was quite satisfied before you arrived."

"Other than being determined to leave."

"But don't you see? Now you've messed that up too." She turned on him, causing him to stop abruptly. There were two steps between them, and she covered half the distance. "Now I don't know what I want. I don't know if I want to go or stay. I don't understand these feelings and I…"

She never finished that sentence. His lips were on hers, and all other thoughts flew out of her mind like birds in flight.

The world tilted, just a little, then righted itself.

Unable to look at him, she stepped away and turned back toward the house. "Why did you do that?"

"Because I wanted to, and I think you wanted me to also."

"Which is beside the point."

"Hey." He tugged on her arm. They were nearly to

the house now, and apparently Gideon hadn't said all that he'd come to say. He pulled her behind the chicken coop so they'd be out of Eunice's sight, who was tinkering with some contraption on the back porch.

"I like you—a lot. And I don't know what's going to happen in six weeks. I don't know if I'll go or if you'll stay. I do know that how I feel about you is different from how I've ever felt about anyone else. I also believe that if we only have six weeks left together, we should spend it getting to know one another. Can't we just explore our feelings and see how this plays out?"

"Wow. That sounds like something you've rehearsed."

"Over and over for the last two weeks." He kissed her again, lightly this time.

She tried not to smile, but it was impossible.

"I'll take that to mean you feel the same."

"I feel something," she admitted. "Something I don't understand. I'd convinced myself I was coming down with a summer cold."

Gideon entwined his fingers with hers, and they resumed walking toward the house.

"Promise you'll stop avoiding me at work?"

She'd thought she'd been subtle about that. She'd even convinced herself that he was avoiding her. "*Ya*. Sure."

"And you'll go out with me this Saturday?"

"You honestly think that's a *gut* idea?"

"I do."

She knew in that moment that the decision she made would affect the rest of the summer, maybe the rest of her life. If she said no, then Gideon would back off and let her be. He was that kind of guy—respectful and not at all pushy. Which made what he'd done today nothing short of courageous. Did he care for her that much?

"Okay." She smiled broadly. "Saturday it is."

"Great. Where should we go?"

"I don't know. How about we talk about it over a pretzel tomorrow?"

"Sounds like a perfect plan."

She pulled her hand out of his as they walked up the porch steps. Eunice must have noticed because she blinked in surprise, looked at Becca and then glanced away. She *had* noticed, but she didn't say anything. If it had been Ada, they'd be peppered with a dozen questions. And if it had been her *dat*...well, she didn't want to think about that. In recent weeks, he'd actually warmed up to her plan to volunteer with MDS, claiming, "You're bound to meet an eligible guy there."

Sarah came out the back door to call Eunice to dinner. Seeing Gideon, she insisted that he stay, as well. Before Becca could wrap her head around all that had happened, they were seated around the family table, enjoying meat loaf, mashed potatoes, corn, salad and fresh bread. After the meal, Sarah insisted on wrapping up some leftovers for Nathan.

Becca walked him out to the buggy, and he kissed her one more time. Her stomach fluttered, and she wished she hadn't eaten dinner after all. Becca had been kissed before, but those kisses had always left her feeling a bit embarrassed and awkward. Those kisses hadn't reached her heart.

Gideon climbed up into the buggy, reminding her of their pretzel date the next day. "And don't forget to keep Saturday open."

"I won't forget."

What else did she have to do?

She watched him drive away and wondered if she'd

just agreed to a very wise or very foolish thing. It could go either way. The one thing she knew for certain was that the lethargy of the last two weeks was gone. In its place was a kind of happiness she couldn't remember experiencing before—and at least a dozen questions about the future.

For now, she decided to ignore the questions.

Gideon couldn't explain what had changed in his attitude. Yes, David's opinion of Shipshe had made him more aware of its good points. David's view of Becca had done the same. Those things, combined with Nathan's gentle counsel, had helped to clear his head. What had he been so afraid of? What was the worst that could happen?

It was possible that he might decide to return to Beeville.

Becca certainly still seemed committed to joining MDS.

But did those things matter as much as *now* mattered?

Right now, they had the opportunity and the desire to be together. Maybe it was time to quit running from his feelings and start investigating them.

And then there was the job. Somehow, over the last six weeks, he'd come to know the market as well as he did the family farm in Beeville. He knew where things were, how to help customers and vendors, even how to change the paper in a cash register. The many visitors who came to the market no longer seemed like an overwhelming crowd. He liked his coworkers, especially the auctioneers. Amos Yoder was a tough but fair boss.

And Becca was, quite simply, someone he wanted to get to know better.

They decided to ride bikes down the Pumpkinvine Trail for their Saturday date. It had been Sarah's suggestion. She'd pulled Gideon aside when she'd seen him at the market on Friday.

"*Gut* weather, *ya*?"

"Sure." He glanced around, wondering why Sarah was talking to him about the weather.

"I hear you and Becca are going out on Saturday."

"She mentioned that?"

"Not exactly. We had to pull it out of her, which is rather like prying a loose tooth from a frightened child. We were trying to make plans, and she was being hedgy."

"Plans?"

Sarah stared at the ground, shaking her head in disbelief. Finally, she looked up at him. "She didn't tell you?"

"Guess not."

"Tomorrow is Becca's birthday."

"What?" The exclamation came out louder than he'd intended. He lowered his voice. "Are you sure?"

"The date of my *schweschder*'s birthday? *Ya*, I'm sure. She finally admitted that she was seeing you on Saturday. We tried to pin her down, but she didn't know the details of your *supposed date*. She seemed a bit unsure about the whole thing."

"She thinks we're being foolish—since one of us will be leaving."

Sarah stared up at the sky, shaking her head, then looked at Gideon and smiled. "Becca wants to be a world traveler, but she wants to be in charge of the itinerary."

"I'm not sure what that has to do with—"

"She's not great with waiting to see how things play out."

"Ah." So she'd shared some of their conversation with

her oldest *schweschder*. He supposed that was normal, since she didn't have a *mamm* to talk it over with.

"I usually make her favorite meal, and then we go to Howie's for ice cream."

"Oh, well, I don't want to intrude on family time."

Sarah was studying him now. She tapped a finger against her lips and then finally shrugged. "Let's do both. You take her to do something outdoorsy. Seems to me she's been feeling a little restless."

"I noticed."

"How about you two bike ride the Pumpkinvine Trail?"

"What's that?"

Sarah explained about the surfaced twenty-five-mile trail that stretched from Shipshewana to Middlebury to Goshen.

"That far?"

"You don't have to ride the entire thing. Afterwards, you can join us for her birthday celebration. How about you drop by our place around one?"

"I didn't exactly bring a bike with me from Texas, and I'm pretty sure Nathan doesn't have one."

Sarah waved that objection away. "You can use *Dat*'s. Bring Becca back home by five, and I'll have dinner ready. Then afterwards, we'll all go to Howie's for ice cream."

He'd envisioned something a little more romantic than a bike ride for their first date, but he hadn't been able to decide exactly what. He'd met her at JoJo's that morning, but they hadn't settled on any specifics for the next day. Mostly, they'd talked about Christmas plans at the market—Christmas plans! In June! He still had a lot to learn in regard to the market, and apparently he also had a lot to learn in regard to Becca.

How had she not mentioned it was her birthday?

Maybe a day out in the sunshine was just what they needed. Later that afternoon, he suggested it to Becca, and she seemed quite enthusiastic about the idea.

When he parked the buggy at her place on Saturday, she was waiting out front, both bikes looking sparkling clean and ready to go. She was wearing an older dress—he could tell because the fabric was a bit faded. Somehow, that only made her look even prettier. He loaded the bikes onto the rack on the back of the buggy, then fastened them with bungee cords that Nathan kept on the back floorboard.

"Is Nathan going to be okay by himself all day?"

"Nathan's off with his buddies. They came by for him before I'd even hitched up Samson."

"He's doing better since you've moved in."

"Really?" Gideon stopped and considered that. "Maybe he is. Could be because he's eating better. He loves to cook."

Ada peeked out through the kitchen window, and he offered a small wave. Sarah joined her and waved as well.

"Is my family watching?"

"Indeed."

"Let's go, then."

"Should I kiss you first?"

"You should not."

He couldn't be offended, since she smiled and blushed the color of a Texas sunset. They were down the lane and out onto the road when he remembered to wish her a happy birthday.

"*Danki*. I'm now twenty-five years old."

Gideon let out a long whistle.

"What?"

"You were just twenty-four, is all."

She swiped at his arm, but he caught her hand and pulled her across the buggy seat so that she was sitting right beside him. The day only got better from there. Becca directed him to a parking area that held two cars and one other buggy. He wound Samson's reins around the hitching post, making sure that the gelding would be waiting in the shade.

The trail wound beside open fields and behind farms, both Amish and *Englisch*. On some sections they'd be alone, and other sections would be crowded with parents pushing baby strollers, kids on Rollerblades and skateboards, and quite a few other bicyclers.

After forty-five minutes, they stopped at a picnic area. Becca had brought a small cooler with drinks and peanut butter sandwiches, which she'd strapped to her bike. They sat at a picnic table and spread out the goods.

"*Danki* for putting this meal together."

"It's only sandwiches, Gideon."

"Sandwiches hit the spot when you've been bicycling for hours on end."

She glanced at her watch, then gave him the stink eye. "Less than an hour."

"Huh. Felt like more. I'm glad you brought me two. I worked up a real appetite."

"You wouldn't rather have cold fried chicken or sliced ham? I thought men were picky about such things."

"I don't care what I eat." He stared down at his second sandwich, then glanced up at her. "It's just nice to spend time with you when we're not trying to catch an escaped goat."

"That little guy made it all the way to the red parking area."

"I thought he wasn't going to stop until he reached the Blue Gate." He finished the sandwich, took a long drink from the bottle of water and then reached for one of the oatmeal cookies. "I didn't expect so many people to be on the trail."

"It's a popular thing. Tourists visit it to see the countryside—"

"And the Amish."

"And the Amish." She nodded in agreement. "Quite a few Plain folks use the trail to travel from home to work and back again."

"Why would they do that?"

"Shipshe to Middlebury is a long distance for a horse, especially when done five days a week. Plus, not all employers have a *gut* place to park a horse for eight hours. So during summer months, some people bike instead. That way, the horse and buggy can stay home in case someone else in the family needs it."

"Bicycling would be cheaper than hiring a driver, I guess."

"They sometimes do that—in the winter. There are a few employers who run a van to various pickup points, and there's also a few *Englisch* drivers who run a taxi service."

"Sounds expensive."

"Not if you split the cost with three or four other workers."

Gideon shook his head in disbelief.

"I know that look. You're about to make a Texas comparison."

"You can't imagine how different it is. Vans and taxis? Paved trails that stretch from one community to another?"

"How do you get around in Beeville? Ride a long-horn?"

He'd told her about the iconic cattle, explaining how large the horns were. She'd laughed, and he could tell that she thought he was exaggerating. "Mostly horse and buggy or walk—but occasionally, we ride the horses. Especially if you're just running down to the general store for an errand or maybe to the post office."

"Like with a saddle or bareback?"

"Saddle. I don't know anyone who enjoys riding bareback. Maybe some folks do at rodeos."

When she asked about those, he only shook his head and said, "You'll have to come and see one. It's not really something I can describe."

He stood, reached for her hands and pulled her to her feet. Glancing around to make sure no one would see them, he kissed her once and then again. She pulled away, laughing and gathering up the items from their picnic.

"What's so funny?"

"You are."

"Meaning?" He tried to look offended, but he couldn't quite pull it off.

"Meaning you're different when you're away from work."

"I'm different when I'm around you." The words came out more seriously than he intended. When she stared at him, wide-eyed, he simply added, "That's a *gut* thing."

Three months ago, if anyone had asked him, he would have said that the perfect summer day was one spent working in the field or caring for the horses. He'd been wrong. The perfect summer day was riding bikes with pretty Becca Yoder in northern Indiana. It occurred to him that this would be a very good way to spend a life.

But was it the life that he wanted to live?

Was it the life she wanted to live?

And could either of them, or both of them, give up what they had thought was their life's dream in order to be together?

Chapter Ten

With five girls in the Yoder family, birthday festivities were relatively modest affairs. They couldn't financially afford a big to-do; and honestly, they were happier with a simpler kind of celebration. A favorite homemade meal, gifts that were usually utilitarian and handmade, and ice cream at Howie's.

When Becca and Gideon arrived back at the farm, she was surprised to see Nathan sitting on the front porch with her *dat*.

"We thought he might like to be included," Sarah explained, turning the chicken that had fried to a golden brown. "*Dat* picked him up an hour ago."

Becca knew Nathan. She knew everyone in their church community, but she'd never spent much time with him. In fact, she'd known his wife better than she did Nathan. Mary had been a sweet thing and a skilled quilter.

It was nice having everyone around the table, with two extra places added for Nathan and Gideon. Nathan was a joke teller, which probably explained why he got along so well with Ada.

"Why couldn't the teddy bear finish his piece of birthday cake?"

Ada started laughing before the punch line.

"Because he was stuffed!" Nathan slapped his knee, and it was impossible not to laugh. The old guy was clearly tickled at his ability to entertain.

Not to be outdone, Ada said, "Better watch out, Becca. Once you're over the hill, you might fall down."

No one had heard that particular sentiment expressed quite that way, but they all nodded as if they understood.

Becca did not feel over the hill, but like many other things that had occurred during the last few weeks, her family's kindness brought tears to her eyes. Their gifts were all spot-on.

Sarah had made her a new dress out of a very light peach-colored fabric. It would be perfect for summer.

Eunice had rigged a small solar panel up to a battery charger. Rechargeable batteries were a big thing in an Amish household, but given that they had no electricity, they had to be recharged at work or via a generator.

"The whole thing folds up like this," Eunice explained. "It'll fit easily in your suitcase and save you tons of money you might have spent on batteries... You know, for flashlights, alarm clocks and even a reading lamp. You're bound to need those things wherever MDS sends you to work."

Bethany gave her a knitted scarf and mittens. The yarn was a variegated dark green and light gray, and a pattern of small Christmas trees had been worked into the edges of the scarf.

"It's lovely, Beth. *Danki*."

Ada rushed from the kitchen and returned, brandishing a bouquet of wildflowers that she'd hidden in a mason jar on the back porch. She didn't have any money to spend since her job at the Blue Gate had lasted less than a week. She'd grown bored standing at the hostess stand and wandered off downstairs to look at the art. When she returned, she'd been given the boot. Turned out that was the third position they'd tried her in. The manager had kindly suggested she try something "a bit more active," since she seemed to have trouble staying in one place and doing her assigned task.

Her *dat* surprised Becca with a suitcase. She hadn't even thought about that. She would need a suitcase if she was going to be traveling with MDS.

"Found it at the thrift store, but it's in very good condition."

"It is. I love it, *Dat. Danki.*"

Nathan gave her a beautiful wooden box—probably five by seven inches and made of maple. "Gideon and I worked on it together," he explained, and then he winked at her, causing everyone to laugh.

"Wait." Sarah tilted her head and squinted her eyes. "Gideon didn't even know it was Becca's birthday until I told him yesterday."

Nathan laughed. "Indeed. I keep a few things back for surprise birthday parties."

Gideon looked a bit nervous as Becca ran her fingertips over the lid of the box.

"Well, open it. I promise there isn't a snake in there."

She opened the box to find it was filled with stationary, stamped envelopes and several pens. She'd stopped and admired them once at Vendor 47's booth. Gideon had been with her that day—in fact, it had been weeks ago. She was surprised and touched that he'd remembered.

"Do you like it?"

"I love it. *Danki*." Gideon's gift touched her heart. They hadn't known each other for very long, but he seemed to understand her. And by giving her the means to write home, he seemed to be reaffirming that he would trust her decision to stay or go.

Had he decided to stay?

They'd avoided the subject. She supposed he'd tell her when he made up his mind, and she would tell him.

"This dinner was delicious, but I suggest we all shout for ice cream." Ada hopped up from her chair and began collecting dishes.

Sarah tried to temper her smile. "It's 'We all *scream* for ice *cream*.' See? They rhyme."

"That's just silly." Ada tossed her *kapp* strings behind her shoulder. "You only scream when you're frightened, like the time Becca nearly stepped on a snake on the porch."

"In my defense, it was rather large."

"No one's scared of ice cream, so I stand by what I said. Let's all shout for ice cream!" As she carried dishes to the kitchen, the rest of the family exchanged looks and smiles.

Becca would miss this if she left. She'd miss Ada's misquoted sayings and her *schweschdern*'s birthdays and her *dat*'s calm and steady guidance. She'd miss the folks from her church community, people who had been around her all her life whom she'd taken for granted—like Nathan.

And she'd miss Gideon.

Fortunately, no one seemed to notice the melancholy turn of her mood. There was much commotion as dishes were cleaned, then washed, dried and put away. She carried glasses into the kitchen and found Eunice flicking soapy water at Gideon, who was holding up a dish towel as if to ward off a thunderstorm. The entire scene struck her as hilarious when she thought of how uncomfortable he'd been in their home that first night he'd eaten with them. Had that really been less than two months ago?

And yet now he seemed so comfortable here.

He seemed at ease with her family, and her family seemed to easily accept him.

Thirty minutes later, they piled into two buggies and made their way to Howie's. Becca sat up front with Gideon, and Nathan sat in the back with Ada.

Gideon was driving behind her *dat*'s buggy since he didn't exactly know the way to the ice-cream shop. "What's the big deal about this ice-cream place?"

"Howie's is an institution here in Shipshe," Becca explained.

"For sure and certain it is," Nathan agreed. "My wife, Mary, insisted on going at least once a month in the summer. She claimed something about the place cheered her spirits."

Ada nodded enthusiastically. "Cheers my spirits. I could eat ice cream morning, noon and night. I could *shout* for ice cream."

Which of course caused everyone to laugh. Gideon glanced at Becca, and he seemed so comfortable and content that she found herself looking at him differently. He really was a nice guy—good-looking, polite and even fun to be around. Plus, he liked her. Was she foolish to walk away from that?

And why couldn't she enjoy one afternoon without worrying about what she was going to be doing six weeks from now?

Ada leaned over the front seat and pointed out the

large sign proclaiming Howie's Ice Cream. It was yellow on top, fading into white, then blue. The word *Howie's* was printed in a stunning blue across the yellow, and the words *Ice Cream* were bright pink.

"Wow. You can definitely see that a ways off."

"Folks come from all over to Howie's—Amish and *Englisch*."

When they pulled into the unpaved parking area, three other buggies and two cars were already there. Becca waved at the other families that were already scattered around the picnic tables. They walked over to the small building, where two Amish teenagers were filling orders.

"Soft serve or hand-dipped cones, shakes and iced coffee. Hmmm." Gideon glanced at her and winked. "I might have found a rival for my JoJo's habit."

"I'm going with pecan praline." Ada worried her thumbnail. "Or strawberry, or maybe rocky road. What are you getting, Eunice? We could switch halfway through."

"Nuh-uh. I'm getting my usual—one scoop of vanilla, one scoop of chocolate—and I'm going to eat every bite."

Sarah chose mint chocolate chip, claiming she could only eat a single scoop. Bethany opted for a small chocolate sundae. "The whipped cream and the cherry are my favorite part."

Becca and Gideon decided to share a banana split.

"That's romantic," Ada declared. "I can't wait until I have a beau to share ice cream with—only he might have to order his own because I really like ice cream."

Becca noticed that her *dat* didn't order anything, claiming that he had a bit of indigestion.

"If you change your mind, we'll share," she told him. "You're okay, right?"

"Right as rain."

He waited at the back of the group so that he could pay for everyone's treats. Nathan tried to hand him some money for his chocolate shake, but Becca's *dat* waved him away. "It's my pleasure, Nathan. We're happy that you and Gideon could join us."

The day was practically perfect.

Becca couldn't remember a happier time, except maybe when her *mamm* had been with them. She sometimes wondered what her *mamm* had been like at her age. Occasionally, she asked Sarah such questions, and her *schweschder* would oblige her with stories that Becca had memorized long ago. Still, sharing those memories was special. A bit of solemnness tempered their boisterous mood as everyone sitting round the table enjoying ice cream realized that there was one important person missing.

Becca's *dat*, never one to avoid a topic if it needed airing, sipped his cup of water and then raised his hand to quiet everyone at the table.

"I would like to say that I think the world of you girls. *Gotte* has blessed me mightily, above all men." His eyes gazed out across the adjacent field. "Above all men."

He seemed to rouse himself from some memory and turned to Becca. "Your *mamm* loved all of you girls, and I truly believe she is watching from heaven, celebrating this day with us." He pulled her close and kissed the top of her head, and Becca felt tears sting her eyes.

There it was again—that overtenderness toward things. Her heart felt almost raw at times. Was it the fact that she was a year older? She'd certainly thought she would have more of the questions about her future figured out by twenty-five. Was it Gideon and her feelings for him? Or was it the thought of leaving, finally leaving this town and her family that meant so much to her? She'd wanted to be free of all that was familiar to her for a very long time, but now that it was within grasp, she felt adrift.

She couldn't sleep that night, so she finally gave up tossing and tiptoed from the room she shared with Eunice, across the living room and out onto the front porch. Gizmo raised his head to look at her, then quickly fell back asleep. Years ago, they'd placed a dog bed against the wall of the porch. In the winter, the sweet old mutt slept in the barn or the mudroom, but this night was warm and beautiful. She rather envied Gizmo his ability to enjoy it.

Becca was sitting there, staring out at the stars, when Sarah joined her.

"Rather late for stargazing."

"I suppose."

She wasn't surprised that Sarah had heard her. Sarah was like the mother hen of the group. No doubt she'd taken on that role when their *mamm* had died. Was that why she'd never married? Her *schweschder* wasn't one to push. She sat there rocking for several minutes, until Becca was again lost in her memories of the last year, the last few weeks, the last day.

Finally, Becca sighed and admitted, "Nothing is like I thought it would be."

"Meaning?"

"Getting older."

"Getting older is exactly as I thought it would be— already my knee hurts at times, and I'm only twenty-eight."

"But nothing makes sense."

"You thought it would?"

"I guess." Becca smiled at herself. It sounded silly when she said it, but it also eased the tightness around her heart. "I thought I couldn't wait to leave, and now I'm not sure I want to go at all. I thought I was so tired of working at the market, but now I think I'll miss it. And Gideon…" She stared out at the stars, grateful that Sarah didn't rush her, didn't jump in with more questions. She simply waited.

"When I first met him, Gideon was difficult and opinionated and so reserved." She felt her face blush. Even in the darkness, she knew her cheeks were stained red. "Now he's rather sweet."

Waiting to be sure she was finished, Sarah stood and said, "I'll be right back."

She was gone a good ten minutes.

"Perhaps my whining scared her off," Becca muttered to the stars.

Sarah returned with two cups of hot tea and a platter of cookies. "I shouldn't want these after the ice cream, but I do."

Sarah moved her chair closer.

"This is your solution for fretfulness and indecision?"

"This is my solution for a troubled heart."

Ouch. Sarah never was one to back away from the truth.

"When do you have to let MDS know your decision?"

"Well, assuming that Gideon agrees to stay—and I'm beginning to think he might—then I should call them by mid-August and be ready to go by the first week of September."

"Okay. So you have a few weeks."

"I do."

"Then on the first weekend in August, you and I will have a sit-down, really hash it out, list the pros and cons, and weigh your choices. The decision is yours, but sometimes it helps to bounce things off another person."

"It does help. *Danki*."

"As for the market…" Sarah sat back in the rocker, cradling her steaming cup of tea. "I've often thought of the market as being like an old dog."

Becca choked on her drink. "A dog?"

"Sure. Rather like Gizmo."

"Meaning what, exactly?"

"You love an old dog. Everyone loves an old dog. He's faithful, you have precious memories of him and he's always been there for you through thick and thin."

"But…"

"But occasionally, even for the best pet owners, the responsibility of owning a dog can wear you down."

"Rather like a horse."

"Exactly. We love our horses, but they are a lot of work."

"So the market is like an old dog…or old horse."

"It's all we've ever known. *Dat* has worked there, in one form or another, since I was born, eventually rising to manager. It's been his lifework. Well, he would say that *we* are his lifework, but you catch my meaning."

"I do."

"I suspect if it were gone tomorrow, if we were to pick up and move somewhere else, then we'd all miss it quite a bit."

"*Ya.* I suppose that's true."

"And that probably makes you feel a bit guilty for wanting to leave it."

Guilty. That was exactly how she felt, and that guilt had been weighing her down.

"Here's the thing, though. The market is *Dat*'s life-work. It doesn't mean it will be ours. It might, or it might not."

Becca blew out a big breath, then confessed to what had been troubling her the most, something she hadn't even realized until this moment. "Am I a bad *doschder* for wanting to go? Shouldn't I…be happy with all of this? Most people would be."

"Every person is different, Becca, and I don't know what *Gotte*'s plans are for you. I do know that Scripture tells us the fruits of His spirit are love, joy, peace…"

"Forbearance and kindness."

"Goodness, faithfulness, gentleness."

"And self-control," they said together, and both laughed. Those Scripture-memorization games they'd played as children had written certain words on their hearts. She was glad for that. Glad she had that firm foundation.

Now Sarah leaned forward and reached for her hands. "The fruit is not guilt or recrimination. *Dat* understands and appreciates your desire to help others, and MDS is a wonderful way to do that."

"Honestly, when I first considered mission work, it wasn't because of my burning love for others. I know that sounds terrible, but it was just a way out of here."

"It is that, but it's also a way to serve. Maybe you haven't realized it, but you have a servant's heart, Becca—whether you're working at the market or on an MDS crew."

The tears slipped down Becca's cheeks then. Some-how, she'd needed to hear those words of affirmation, needed to know that her family was really pulling for her, not just tolerating her absurd and unusual plans.

Sarah stood and walked to the door. Before opening it, she turned around, walked back and squatted in front of Becca. Then she addressed the one item that they hadn't discussed. "As for Gideon, he seems like a super nice guy. But *nice guy* doesn't cut it, you know? The person that you fall in love with, he needs to be the one person you can't imagine yourself living without."

"Not to set the bar too high."

"Set the bar high, Becca. You're worth it."

And with that, Sarah was gone, leaving Becca to watch the stars and wonder.

Gideon was barely aware of the fact that the end of his second month had come and gone. He was now handling the market alone. It wasn't a problem. Actually, it helped to be doing it alone. His days were busy, he didn't have any time to kill and he knew what was expected of him. He even handled the July Fourth holiday weekend on his own.

Amos was impressed and told him so. "I know you're still undecided, but you have a definite talent for this work."

"I appreciate your saying that."

"You know me well enough to trust I wouldn't say it unless it was true." Amos grimaced and pressed a hand to his chest.

"Are you okay?"

"Probably that second cup of coffee I had."

Gideon had made it to the office door when he found the courage to turn around and ask, "Has Becca shared her plans with you?"

When Amos sat back and crossed his arms, Gideon rushed to amend his question. "I'm not asking you to betray anything said in confidence. It's just that she hasn't mentioned it to me at all, and if I bring up the topic, she quickly changes it."

Instead of answering, Amos laughed. "When Becca was only three, she told her *mamm* that she was going to be a doctor so that she could take care of her baby dolls. Then, when she was five, she'd decided to be a veterinarian because we had a horse with a split hoof that needed extra tending."

"High aspirations."

"She has a tender heart, and she's definitely goal oriented. She always has been. I'm not sure what Becca will decide, but I am sure that she will figure out what's best and follow that path."

Amos reached for his glasses, donned them and pulled a stack of invoices toward him, indicating the conversation was done. But as Gideon retraced his steps down the hall, he realized Amos hadn't exactly answered the question.

Becca was rarely at the market now. He called the phone shack or stopped by to see her if he had a question, but she'd trained him well, so that didn't happen often. He'd managed to take care of ordering the vast amount of Christmas supplies they would need—hot chocolate, candy canes, tins of cookies, several sets of new lights and even sleigh bells. He had a hard time envisioning the market during the holidays. What would it be like? Would there be snow? Would he miss his family?

Was he staying?

He and Becca still went out together on Saturdays, and while he thought of those times as dates, he wasn't sure if she did. Since the Saturday of her birthday, she'd been more serious, quieter, and he often caught her studying him.

Gideon knew that he needed to make his decision independent of hers. Perhaps that was the ticket. Perhaps she was waiting on him to decide. But would his decision to stay make *her* want to stay? Or would it simply give her the assurance that things would be okay so that she could decide to leave?

Respect. Love. Priorities.

He did respect Becca. He was amazed at what a smart and compassionate person she was.

Did he love her? Maybe. More importantly, he thought that Nathan had been referring to a different type of affection—not romantic love, necessarily. Maybe he'd been speaking of the long-term abiding love you had for a family member, or your neighbor or a friend. Possibly what he felt for Becca was all those things.

The one thing he was certain of was that what he felt for her went far beyond anything he'd experienced before, but it had started there. It had started with caring for her as a friend and coworker.

Which left priorities. His priority at the moment was to run the market, to fulfill his commitment to his parents and to do right by Amos.

Two days later, he had the most challenging day at the market to date. An owner of one of the lots to be auctioned changed his mind, so the merchandise had to be pulled and returned. Two of the market's animals escaped the Backyard Barnyard. With *Englischers* laughing and snapping pictures, he'd managed to capture both the goat and the sheep and return them to their pens. He felt ridiculous walking back, holding one under each arm, but he also felt a bit triumphant. A goat and a sheep couldn't get the best of him.

One vendor ran out of change, another couldn't get a Wi-Fi signal and was unable to process sales, and a third got into an argument with a customer who thought his prices were unfair. Gideon had sent an auctioneer who had a free hour to the bank to exchange a hundred dollars for rolls of change; he'd shown the vendor how to take payments by hand and record them so that he could process them later; and he'd negotiated a compromise on the price of raw honey, throwing in a five-dollar voucher to the market's snack shop.

He'd handled it all, and he'd enjoyed it.

He felt satisfied, content, sure.

That afternoon, before leaving, he called his parents and shared his decision. He would stay. His one caveat was that he wanted to come home for a week in mid-September. The market officially closed after Labor Day, though they were still open on special holidays and for certain auctions. The rush of summer would be over, and Amos would do fine without him for such a short time.

His parents agreed and congratulated him on his decision. He noted a tone of pride in their voices, and although he'd often been cautioned that pride was a sin, it made him happy. He wanted his parents to be proud of him. He wanted to be the man that they had raised him to be.

As he hung up the phone, he reminded himself that by agreeing to take the job permanently, he could be effectively sending Becca away. If that was what she wanted, then he'd find a way to live with it. He loved her, and he would continue to love her regardless of how many miles were between them.

He walked out of his office—wasn't it strange to call it that?—and saw Amos's door still open at the end of the hall. Glancing at his watch, he was surprised to see it was past seven. Amos rarely stayed so late. He'd told Gideon once that he took his responsibilities as a father seriously, and eating dinner with his family was an important part of that responsibility. Plus, he enjoyed being home with his family.

"One day, they'll all have flown the nest, and I'll be an old man, wondering how that happened." He'd laughed and added, "If at least one would settle down and marry, I believe the rest might follow."

So why was he still in his office?

Gideon walked down the hall, calling out to Amos, expecting to hear his hearty reply. But when he pushed through the partially open door, what he found was Amos bent over his desk, clutching his heart.

Chapter Eleven

Becca rushed through the Goshen Health Hospital doors, followed quickly by her four *schweschdern*. And that moment was when Gideon admitted to himself that he was well and truly in love with Rebecca Yoder, because he would have done absolutely anything to erase the look of grief on her face.

He stood as all five of Amos's *doschdern* rushed over to where he was waiting with Bishop Ezekiel.

"Is he okay?"

"Can we see him?"

"What happened, exactly?"

Ezekiel held out a hand and patted the air, as if he could soothe their worries with a gesture. "He's stabilized. You can't see him yet, and no one is exactly sure what happened. Gideon found him."

The five women turned their attention to Gideon. Sarah, Becca, Eunice, Bethany and Ada—all waiting on him to explain this terrible thing that had happened. All waiting on him to calm their fears.

He pulled in a deep breath and ran a hand through his hair. "I'd finished up in the office." He didn't add that he'd just finished calling his parents before going to see Amos. He didn't think a hospital waiting room was the place to share the news that he'd decided to stay permanently.

"I saw Amos's door open and wondered why he was still there, since he usually leaves in time to be home for dinner. He was at his desk, clutching his chest. I assumed it was his heart."

"But he was okay?"

"His color was quite pale, and he was having trouble breathing. When the paramedics arrived, they gave him a nitroglycerin tablet and put an oxygen mask over his face. He pulled it off long enough to tell me to contact you girls."

"Just like *Dat* to worry about us," Sarah noted.

"But he's okay? Right? Because if something happened to him…" Ada dissolved into a flood of tears. Sarah put an arm around her and guided her over toward two chairs. She spoke softly to her, reassuring her that they would weather this as a family. Gideon noticed then that the two were praying together.

Ezekiel saw it, too, because he raised his eyebrows and said, "*Gut* idea, *ya*?" They formed a circle, and as they did, Sarah and Ada rejoined the rest of the family. Ezekiel prayed for the doctors and nurses, for the family, and for Amos. He thanked *Gotte* that Gideon had been there, found Amos and called for help. He asked for *Gotte*'s blessing upon the paramedics who had provided emergency care. He ended with, "*Danki* for caring for us, Oh Lord—more even than you care for the sparrow. Amen."

When Gideon opened his eyes, he raised his gaze to Becca's. Tears were sliding down her face, but she attempted a smile. After that, the family collapsed into chairs. Gideon wasn't sure where to go, whether he should even stay, but then Becca looked up and patted the chair next to her. It was all the encouragement he needed.

She reached for his hand and clasped it in hers. "If you hadn't been there, if you hadn't called 911, *Dat* might... he might..."

"Let's not worry about what might have happened. Okay?"

"*Ya.* You're right." She looked around the waiting room as if she still couldn't believe she was there. "How did you get here?"

"Uber. I called Ezekiel right after the paramedics arrived. He was on his way home and turned around to come back to the market. I wanted to take Nathan's buggy out to your place, but he said that we should call a driver and follow the ambulance. It was his idea to have one of the deacons come out and tell you." Gideon crossed, then uncrossed his arms. "I would have felt better telling you myself."

"*Nein.* Ezekiel was right. Knowing that you were already here, that you and Ezekiel were able to answer any questions the doctors might have had..." Her eyes darted around the room, and she rubbed her palms against the apron she wore. Finally, she leaned forward, elbows on her legs, head practically between her knees.

"Are you all right?"

"*Nein.*"

"Can I do anything?"

"*Nein.*"

Gideon didn't know what else to ask or what to say, so he simply sat there beside her. When someone mentioned coffee, he hopped up, meandered around the hospital halls and finally found a vending machine. He reentered the waiting room with three cups and would have gone back for more, but at that moment, a doctor came out, looking for the Yoder family.

He thought to move away and give them their privacy. After all, he wasn't technically family. He was a coworker and employee. Other than that, he couldn't have said what his role was here. Best to hang back and not intrude. He set down the cups of coffee on a small table as all five Yoder *schweschdern* and Ezekiel moved toward the doctor.

Becca glanced back over her shoulder, saw Gideon and retraced her steps. "Come on. I want you with us."

So it was he found himself once again within that circle of the Yoder family—as welcome and needed as the bishop. How had he become so close to this family in such a short time? Why was it that they felt like his own family? In some ways, he thought he knew them better than he did his own *schweschder* and *bruders*.

The doctor was an older woman, with gray hair and a compassionate expression. "I'm Dr. Marjorie Clark, and I'm caring for your father. Mr. Yoder is doing as well as can be expected. He experienced a myocardial infarction."

"What's that?" Eunice asked.

"It's a heart attack, dear." The doctor peered over her glasses at the group. "It's very fortunate that you found him and called 911 when you did. We've stabilized him, and now I'd like to run some tests."

"What kind of tests?" Sarah asked.

The doctor explained about cardiac caths, angioplasty and stents. As she answered those questions, Gideon had a sense of being in a dream. It was almost as if he'd had this exact conversation before. Then he remembered his *onkel*, and the family convening in a Corpus Christi hospital.

He remembered it had been a long road to recovery, complete with days of remarkably better health and then other days of painful setbacks. Gideon understood that Amos had a disease. It wasn't like breaking a leg or needing stitches for a cut. It was something that he would have to live with and manage for the rest of his life.

The family looked somewhat stunned at all the doctor had said, but they nodded in agreement. Gideon was suddenly glad that he'd been through this before, that he knew a little of what lay ahead—and most importantly, that he had already made his decision to stay before this happened.

The question was, when should he tell Becca? Because on the one hand, now did not seem like the time. On the other hand, it would be one less thing for her to worry about. Then the doctor left, and the girls flopped back into their chairs, all chattering at once, and he knew that it wasn't the right time.

Two more couples came through the hospital doors—both apparently close to the Yoder family. Gideon recognized Benjamin Mast and his wife—Samuel's parents. The other couple he'd seen at church, but he couldn't recall their names. Everyone nodded hello, and Ezekiel caught them up on Amos's condition.

Sarah rushed off to call someone. Eunice sat close to Ada. They both looked suddenly young and in need of a father. That made sense. Their father was their rock. He held their family together—guided them, provided for them and lived out his faith in a way that they could see and follow.

Bethany had a bag slung over her shoulder, and she pulled out a knitting project. When she caught him watching, she explained, "It helps to keep my hands busy."

"I'd end up with three arms in a sweater or two holes in a hat." Becca pressed her fingers to her closed eyes. "My thoughts are jumping all over the place."

"Well, this is a blanket for a new *boppli*. It's an easy pattern, so there's little chance I'll make a mistake." Then Bethany's bottom lip began to quiver, and tears slipped down her cheeks.

Gideon jumped up and fetched one of the now-cold cups of coffee. "Here. Maybe this will help."

She nodded her thanks and dutifully took a large sip, scowling at the taste, which caused them all to laugh. And that laughter seemed to break the tension in the room.

Becca smiled for the first time since she'd rushed through the hospital doors. "We're together. That's what matters. That's what *Mamm* would want if she were here. Dr. Clark seems to know what she's doing."

"Oh, *ya*, for sure," Benjamin Mast spoke up. "Dr. Clark took care of me when I had my heart attack. She's the cat's meow."

Mrs. Mast nodded in agreement as she pulled out her own knitting. "She was able to handle Benjamin, and he's almost as stubborn as Amos. Your *dat* is going to be just fine."

Instead of sounding like empty words of encouragement, the fact that the Masts had been through a similar tragedy and were here to talk about it bolstered everyone's mood. Perhaps that was what neighbors were for. Maybe that was why they'd come—because they remembered the waiting and the fears and the loneliness of having a loved one going through a medical emergency.

And then Gideon realized how glad he was that he was still here, that he hadn't gone back to Texas, that he was able to help Becca and her family—even in small ways like fetching coffee and sitting beside her. Texas would always be his home; the land and the people had made him who he was. But Indiana? Indiana was where his heart was, and it was also—he hoped—where his future waited.

Becca couldn't believe all that had happened in the last week.

Her *dat* had returned home four days after the ambulance whisked him away to the hospital. She was so grateful to have him back with them that at times, it felt as if her heart hurt. Though she hadn't done so since she was a child, she now knelt beside her bed every evening—thanking *Gotte* for his mercies, asking for his help, basking in his care.

Dr. Clark had determined that her *dat* needed a stent, medicine and less stress. The stent had been inserted two days after his heart attack. He'd begun the medicine at the hospital, and Sarah had filled the prescriptions so he could continue them at home. The doctor and nutritionist had given them several pages of instructions.

What he could do and when.

Things he should wait to do, not attempting them until he was fully recovered.

What to eat and what not to eat.

How to manage cardiovascular disease so that he could live a long and full life.

Doctor appointments were added to the family calendar, which hung from a hook in the kitchen.

Sarah took care of modifying everyone's diet. "We should have been eating this way for years—it only makes sense when you read the health guidelines." This was her favorite refrain as she put more vegetables and less meat on the dinner table. Desserts even took on a whole new look, with more fruit and cookies made with honey instead of refined sugar. She began experimenting with different types of bread using whole grains.

Becca felt as if she were a horse some days. "I'm probably getting more oats than you are," she confessed to Oreo and Peanut. Both mares simply nodded their heads and nudged her apron pocket for their piece of carrot.

As for making sure that her *dat* experienced less stress, that was more difficult to achieve every day, because every day he seemed to feel better.

She knew that he was grateful for their care, but he'd never been one to sit around when there was work to be done. Dr. Clark had warned them that with men—especially Amish men—convincing them to slow down could be the hardest part.

"He needs a few weeks off to let his body heal."

"For sure and certain." Sarah's expression and demeanor were quite serious. In fact, it was a waste of time and energy to contradict her when she was completely set on a thing, and Becca knew that her *schweschder* was very set on her *dat* following the doctor's orders.

"He can work, but not twelve-hour days," Dr. Clark had cautioned.

"I'll make sure he limits his time at the market to

eight hours," Becca said. "If I have to, I'll lock him out of his own office."

"And I want him to keep his follow-up appointments. That's critical. It would be best if one of you came with him. I like to keep the family involved."

"We want to be involved," Eunice assured her. "One of us will be there."

Ada seemed to be having the hardest time with their *dat*'s illness. One afternoon, as they took laundry down from the lines and folded it, Becca asked her how she was doing.

"I always thought of him as too big to fail."

"I believe you're referring to *Englisch* banks."

"I'm just a kid. I still need my *dat*."

"You're not a kid—you're a grown woman, and we all need *Dat*. He's going to be okay, Ada."

"He can't turn over the bucket. He just can't." She looked at Becca with tears in her eyes.

Becca once again felt pressure and pain in her heart. Was she simply experiencing sympathy pain for her others? Or was she suddenly aware of how precious her family was to her—how much she needed them?

She put her arms around her *schweschder* and let her have a *gut* cry. Since she was the youngest, they'd always coddled Ada. Now she was having to grow up, and she was having to do so quickly. On top of everything else, Becca felt quite conflicted. She'd gone back to work at the market. Gideon was doing a fabulous job, but he couldn't handle all the day-to-day operations on his own. She hadn't given up on her dream of serving with MDS, though. The difference was that now she felt an increasing burden of guilt when she thought of it.

Becca and Ada had just walked into the house with

the baskets of laundry when she heard her *dat* calling for her.

"One minute." Becca set the basket down in the living room, then hurried to the back porch.

Sarah had made him a sort of workroom under the porch roof. She'd put in a few tables, made sure there was a comfortable chair and even given him a bell, which he absolutely refused to use. "I'm not a cat." That comment only made sense to Sarah and Becca, as they were old enough to remember the old tomcat they'd had. He had been a great mouser but often got underfoot. The small bell they'd hung around the tabby's neck had easily solved the problem.

Their *dat*'s mood improved when he was involved with the market, and being outside in the fresh air seemed to help too.

"Tell me about the market."

So she did. She told him that numbers were up for the summer over last year, vendors were already asking for the forms to sign up for the holiday weekends, and Christmas supplies had been delivered and stocked.

Amos ran his fingers through his beard. "We might be able to step things up a bit at Christmas."

"*Dat*, you're supposed to do less, not more."

"But since Gideon is staying, I'll have plenty of help. You know how many *Englischers* come to town over the holidays. We could set up a living manger scene or a…"

Becca's mind had stopped with the comment about Gideon, and she realized she was standing there with her mouth wide-open. "What did you just say?"

"That we could have a living manger scene—what the French call a *crèche*."

Her mouth was suddenly dry, and she blinked her

eyes rapidly, as if she'd be able to clear her vision and see the thing that wasn't making any sense. "About Gideon. What did you say about Gideon?"

"Oh. That he's staying. I thought you knew."

She gingerly moved a stack of papers to the small table, then perched on the chair beside her *dat*. "I wasn't aware that he was staying. He hasn't mentioned it to me. I know you must be happy about that."

"I'm inordinately pleased."

"But do you think…that is, I would hate for Gideon to make such a decision because of your illness. He might, well, he might regret it later."

Her *dat* cocked his head, studied her a minute, and then reached out and patted her hand. "You really have grown up, haven't you, Becca? Those are wise words indeed, and in fact, I was worried that you might decide to stay because of my illness. I was concerned that such a decision made in haste might be one you regret later."

She was shaking her head before he'd even finished. "I haven't decided what I'm going to do, *Dat*, but when I do, it'll be for the right reasons. It's something I'm still praying about."

"Gut."

"But Gideon…"

He waved away her concerns. "Gideon was coming to my office to tell me his decision when he found me having a heart attack."

"Umm…could he just be saying that? To make you feel better?"

"He could, I suppose." Now he removed his glasses, cleaned them with a cloth that he kept in his pocket, put them back on and smiled. "But he'd called his parents before he came to tell me. They wrote me a letter that very night, saying how pleased they are. I have it here somewhere, if you'd like to read it."

"*Nein.* That's not necessary." She stood and moved the stack of invoices back to the chair. When she was at the door, she turned back to him. "I'm going to take the buggy out for a few minutes. Is that all right?"

"Certainly. Dr. Clark hasn't cleared me to drive yet. When she does, you can be sure I won't be lounging around the back porch."

Becca stopped in the kitchen and told Sarah not to hold the meal for her; then she hurried out to the barn without even checking her reflection in the mirror. She'd worked all day at the market, rushed home, worked in the garden a half hour and then helped with laundry. She probably looked rumpled, tired and a little dirty. That was okay with her. She *felt* rumpled and tired and a little dirty. She also felt more than a little irritated because she had worked closely with Gideon the last two days. He hadn't mentioned a word of his decision to her.

She'd thought they were friends.

She'd thought they might even be more than that.

And friends didn't withhold things from each other.

Gideon Fisher had some explaining to do.

Chapter Twelve

Gideon had been home less than an hour when he heard the clatter of a buggy coming down Nathan's lane.

"Sounds like company." Nathan was helping Gideon muck out Samson's stall. Actually, he was watching more than helping, but the old guy seemed to enjoy their time spent doing chores together.

Stepping out of the barn, Gideon was surprised to see Becca. He hurried over and arrived beside the driver's door as she said "Whoa" to their younger mare, Peanut. The horse was a light tan color and seemed to have enjoyed the dash over to Nathan's place.

"Is everything okay?"

"*Ya, Dat*'s fine." Becca set the brake, hopped out of the buggy and stood there glaring at him, both hands propped on her hips. Boy, did that look take him back. He was fairly sure Becca had confronted him with the exact same tone and body language the first day he'd worked at the market—and a few times after that as well. He almost laughed because he understood it was what she did when she was uncertain about a thing, not when she was angry.

"Great. I'm glad you came to visit. If I'd have known, I would have…"

"Why didn't you tell me?"

"Tell you…"

"That you were staying." She actually stomped her foot. "How could you not tell me, Gideon?"

"Oh, that."

"Yes, that."

Nathan waved at her as he carried a bucket of oats out to Samson. Becca waved back, then turned her attention back to Gideon with renewed irritation.

"Does he know too? Did you tell everyone except me? Do I really mean so little to you?"

"Hang on a minute." He reached out his hand and placed it on her hand. He wanted to pull her into his arms, tell her how much he cared, ask her to be his bride. He didn't do any of those things, though. He'd matured enough to be able to tell the difference between impulsive actions and wise ones.

She stared at his hand, then up at him—head cocked, lips pursed, eyes blazing.

"Let's just sit down and talk."

"I don't want to sit down." She crossed her arms, trying mightily to hold on to her anger.

"We'll walk, then. Will Peanut be okay?"

"*Ya.* Sure. She doesn't mind waiting."

Peanut was already cropping on grass. Gideon wound her lead rope around the hitching post positioned outside Nathan's barn, then snagged Becca's hand. She sent him another cross look. He smiled, and she squinted her eyes, her lips forming a straight, tight line.

"Wow. Okay. I can see you're upset. Let's walk over

to Nathan's west field. There are some pretty wildflowers there."

"I didn't come to see wildflowers. I came for answers."

"Indeed. Yes, I can tell."

As he led her to the other side of Nathan's property where they could have a bit of privacy, he told her about the week before, how well things had gone, how he'd finally felt as if he belonged at the market.

"I knew you'd be *gut* at my job." She was still frowning—still sulking, actually.

"I'm *gut* at it because you taught me well, and your *dat*—well, he's created a *gut* place to work, a smoothly running organization."

"And you really want to stay?"

They'd reached the field, and she'd bent to gather some of the flowers—blue phlox, indigo and asters. The field was resplendent with color, and he'd wanted to show it to her. Now he waited for her to look up at him. She did, eventually, but she still clutched the flowers, as if they were a lifeline between her old life and this new one.

"Yes, I really want to stay. I had phoned my parents the evening of your *dat*'s heart attack. I called them, told them my decision and intended to tell your *dat* the next day. Then I saw his office door open..."

He let the rest of that sentence drift away on the summer breeze. They both knew what had happened after that. The last week had passed in a flurry of emotions for both of them.

"You're sure? You're sure you decided before you found him?"

"*Ya.* I am. Look at me, Becca." He waited and finally she met his gaze. Gideon reached out and touched her face. "I'm staying because this job is a *gut* fit for me, and I like working for your *dat*. Also, in case you haven't figured it out, I'm in love with you."

"You are?" Her eyes had widened, and the words came out as the faintest of whispers.

"I am." He almost laughed that he could be so sure. "I decided not to tell you just yet because I realized you're still struggling with your decision regarding MDS."

"Oh." Tears filled her eyes, and she abruptly turned away.

"That's exactly what I didn't want—to make you cry." He waited a moment, not wanting to push her.

She turned and continued a slow trek through the wildflowers, and he followed—thinking that he loved the way she felt things so strongly, the way she expressed her feelings, even the way she handled her anger and confusion. He loved every single thing about Becca Yoder. She might not be perfect, but neither was he. Perfection didn't matter. She was the person that he wanted to share his life with.

When she'd crossed half the field to the large maple tree, she plopped onto the ground.

"Why didn't you want to tell me either of those things? About your decision to stay and about…"

"Loving you?"

She nodded.

"Because my decision is independent of yours." He sat beside her and took his time with his answer, choosing his words carefully. "The last thing I want you to feel is more pressure. Love isn't about pressuring the other person. It's about accepting them."

"When did you become so wise?" She swiped at her

eyes, leaving bits of flower blossoms stuck to her fore-head and *kapp*.

Gideon reached forward and brushed them away.

He again fought the urge to take her in his arms. He knew now wasn't the time. He could wait. He'd wait as long as it took.

"I believe this fresh, cool Indiana air has made me a wiser, more mature person. Could be that the Texas sun was stunting my emotional growth."

She shook her head at the absurdity of his answer, then hiccupped and swiped at more tears.

"I never used to cry so easily."

"That's okay. Six months ago, tears would have sent me running for the hills. I didn't know what to do with a crying woman."

"And now you do?"

"Not really."

The sun was nearly to the horizon, and Gideon thought that Becca—sitting there under the tree, sur-rounded by wildflowers and the pastel colors of a sum-mer's sunset—just might be the most beautiful thing he'd ever seen.

He cleared his throat. "You don't have to worry about the market. I will be here to take care of things. I like that you came back to help this week. I like working with you, but if you still decide your place is with MDS, you won't hear any argument from me."

That had been hard for him. He'd somehow thought that he should fight for the woman he loved, but Nathan had set him straight on that notion. "Love is given—freely. All you need to do is care for the person, be pa-tient and trust."

The memory of those words caused him to inch closer

until they were sitting side by side, their backs against the tree, watching the sun dip below the horizon.

"I don't know what to do." Becca's voice was soft, but it was no longer wobbly.

"That's okay."

"I don't even know what I want to do."

"Kind of the same thing."

"I care about you, too, Gideon."

"That's *gut* to hear."

He'd known that already. He could tell every time she looked at him—well, except when she was aggravated… But even then, her entire being seemed tinged with affection.

He had no doubt about how Becca felt, but he understood that she'd cherished her dream of traveling for a very long time. He wasn't going to ask her to give up something that meant so much to her. If it meant that they would be separated, he'd find a way to survive that. The one thing he was sure of was that when she did return home, he'd be waiting. It might be several months. It might even be Christmas or the new year or next summer, but the timing didn't matter. Becca was worth waiting for.

Becca might have dithered back and forth over her decision for a very long time, but the week after that conversation with Gideon, she received a phone call at work.

There had been floods on the East Coast. MDS was sending crews to North Carolina.

Could she go? Could she leave immediately?

"Maybe. I'm not sure. Can I call you back?"

She'd walked down the hall in something of a daze. Her *dat* was back at work, though the entire family was monitoring his work hours closely to ensure he didn't overdo it.

He looked up as soon as she walked into the office. When she shut the door, he sat back and took off his reading glasses.

"Problem?"

"I don't know."

"There's something you need to talk about, then."

"Ya." She sank into the chair opposite him. "MDS just called. The flooding on the East Coast has left many people with severely damaged homes. They're sending crews, and they want to know if I can go—immediately."

Her *dat* closed the folder in front of him, set his glasses perpendicular to the folder and finally looked up at her.

"Do you want to go?"

"I don't know if I'm ready," Becca admitted.

"You've been ready—for a long time, I think."

Becca glanced around the office, as if she could see the entire market grounds and all the people through the walls. In a way, she could. She could picture this place in her sleep. What she couldn't picture was missing out on the Labor Day Market Weekend or the Day after Thanksgiving Horse Sale or the Christmas festivities. She couldn't imagine not seeing Gideon every day or not being there to check on her father.

But this was her chance. Was she really going to turn it down? When she returned her gaze to her *dat*, he was smiling.

"I'm fine, *doschder*. You don't have to worry about me. And Gideon is staying. Your duties here are covered. You're free to go."

How long had she waited to hear those words?

And yet now they filled her with as much dread as excitement.

"What if something happens? What if you need me?"

"The buses run both ways." He stood, walked around the desk and sat in the chair next to her. "We will miss you, but this day has been a long time coming."

"I was going to wait—after your heart problems, I'd made up my mind to wait."

"But it's not necessary. Dr. Clark is taking *gut* care of me, and with your *schweschdern* watching my every move, there's little chance I'll eat wrong, miss a doctor's appointment or overdo it here at work." He reached out and patted her head. "It's your turn, Becca. Go and do what you've dreamed of for so long—and when you're ready, come home. You will always be welcome at home."

"Right. Okay." She jumped up, then sat back down. "Is it okay for me to leave now? I need to go to the bank and withdraw some money, stop by the general store to purchase a few supplies, and call the MDS coordinator back."

"Take the buggy. I'll catch a ride home with Gideon or one of the other workers."

Gideon.

Should she tell him? Of course she should. Where was he?

She hurried back to her office, returned the phone call to the MDS coordinator and confirmed that she could leave the next day. She wrote down the instructions for what bus station she should arrive at and the phone number for the local MDS crew leader. She added *Buy Ticket* to her growing list of to-do items.

This was bizarre.

Was she really considering leaving tomorrow morning? Becca stuffed the note with the MDS information into her purse, looped the strap over her shoulder and snatched up her to-do list.

She dashed out of the office and hurried across the market grounds to find Gideon. He was supposed to be working in the auction barn, supervising the customer pickup area, but she couldn't find him in the auction area. He wasn't in the auction office either. Where was he?

James hurried past her, and she called out to him.

"I'm looking for Gideon. Any idea where I can find him?"

"He's out in the red parking area, helping some gent load what he purchased into a cattle trailer."

But when she arrived at the parking lot, an *Englischer* with a large white truck and matching cattle trailer was pulling out onto the main road. She spun in a circle. No Gideon in sight. She'd somehow managed to miss him.

She glanced at her watch.

She needed to go. Walking back across the market, finding Gideon, talking to him, then returning to her buggy would take at least half an hour. She looked at her watch again, did the math and knew that she needed to leave. Hopefully, she would see him tonight.

Her first stop was at the bank. She withdrew what she hoped was enough for the bus ticket and her first week in North Carolina. If she needed more money once she was there, she could use her debit card. Her next stop was to purchase her bus ticket. The person working at the window was very helpful. "We can get you there, but you'll have to leave on our first bus."

"What time is that?"

"Six thirty in the morning, and don't be late. Our

drivers have a tight schedule. They can't afford to wait for anyone."

"I won't be late."

Peanut seemed quite happy to be driven to and fro. Becca stopped at the general store, then at the grocery store, and finally made it home.

"You're early," Sarah said. She'd been sweeping the porch, and now she stood there, half leaning on the broom and looking at Becca with a mildly amused expression. "Is there a barn on fire?"

"*Nein*. Not exactly."

Now Sarah's eyebrows arched up. "Another type of emergency?"

"Sort of." Becca juggled her packages. "Do you think you could ask Eunice to unharness Peanut for me?"

"She's coming from the barn now."

Becca turned to see Eunice walking toward them, wiping her hands on an old rag. "Everything okay at the market?"

"Yes." Becca stood there, a bag in both arms, halfway between her *schweschdern*. Swallowing, she looked from one to the other. "I'm going to North Carolina, with MDS, at six thirty tomorrow morning."

She would look back on that evening with an equal mix of gratitude and wonder. Sarah went into full-on emergency mode. She sent Eunice to unharness Peanut. Bethany was recruited to help Becca pack clothing and toiletries. Sarah made a list of necessary items and then optional items. "What doesn't fit, we can mail to you, or you can buy it there."

Ada wandered in, flush with news. "I got the job!" She squealed and spun in a circle. "I'm going to be a teacher's apprentice. I just know I'm going to love it."

Becca and her *schweschdern* stopped what they were doing and enfolded Ada in a hug.

Oh, how I'll miss this.

Ada pulled away and looked at the chaotic scene in the living room. "What's going on? Is someone moving out, or is someone moving in?"

"I'm going to North Carolina tomorrow to work with MDS."

Ada's mouth opened in a perfect O, and then she shook her head and said, "We best get popping, then. What can I do to help?"

By the time Amos arrived home, Becca's suitcase was packed and lying open beside her bed. All that was left to do in the morning was to get dressed, then store her toothbrush and nightgown in the suitcase. On top of her clothes were her Bible and Nathan's box holding the stationery that Gideon had given her.

"Where's Gideon?" she asked, dashing out the front door when she heard the clatter of buggy wheels.

But it wasn't Gideon who had driven her *dat* home. Samuel Mast waved at Becca, then drove away. Her *dat* climbed the porch steps. Taking in her expression, he reached for her hand. "Let's sit a minute."

"What happened? Is he okay?"

"Gideon is fine. He left a note, which wasn't delivered to me until you'd already gone. Nathan had a medical appointment over in South Bend. It's a regular appointment—not an emergency. He hires an *Englisch* driver to take him and bring him back. Usually one of his friends accompany him, but his friend had to cancel so—"

"So Gideon went with him. Okay. That makes sense. I guess I can go over after dinner."

"It's an overnight test."

"What?"

"He had to check in tonight. They hook him up to some monitors, and they finish up by noon tomorrow. I don't know any other details."

"Oh." Becca's mind went blank.

Her *dat* waited.

"So I won't be able to tell Gideon goodbye."

When she didn't move to go inside, didn't say anything else or even pull her gaze away from the buggy trundling down their lane, he patted her hand. "I know that you and Gideon have grown quite close. I understand you would have liked to say goodbye in person, but I believe he will understand this situation. He'll know that you tried."

She only stared at him, wondering what she was doing and if she could bear leaving Shipshewana without speaking to Gideon first.

"You can write him a nice letter. We'll be sure he gets it. Unless you're having second thoughts about going."

That pulled her from her reverie like cold water splashed in her face. "*Nein.* I'm not having second thoughts."

They walked inside together.

Sarah had thrown together a simple supper of sandwiches and soup. Becca knew she should eat, but she only managed a few bites. She was about to leave, to go upstairs and bathe and wash her hair—the very last things on Sarah's list—when her *dat* cleared his throat.

"I think we should have a time of prayer for Becca."

They joined hands around the table. Her father prayed for her trip, that she would be a blessing to those she met; that *Gotte* would provide for her, watch over her and keep her in His tender care. *Amen*s circled the table, and everyone, even her *dat*, fumbled for napkins to wipe their eyes.

It was Ada who saved the day. "They say absence makes the heart grow fainter, but I feel faint already, and you're not even gone."

Their tears were replaced with laughter, followed by the business of cleaning the kitchen and evening chores.

Becca paused a moment to drink it all in, to remember each person in her family as they were now. Then she went upstairs, pulled out a sheet of Gideon's stationery and sat down to write him a letter.

Chapter Thirteen

Nathan's medical test went well. They dismissed the old guy with instructions that he "Keep doing whatever it is you're doing."

Gideon had a slight crick in his neck from sleeping in the hospital chair, but he was eager to get back to the market. He dropped Nathan off at home, changed clothes and accepted the sandwich Nathan pushed into his hands. *"Danki."*

"Gem gschehne."

It was a beautiful August day—nothing like what he'd be enduring in Texas in August. Back home, the temperatures always hovered near the 100-degree mark, and rain in late summer was rare. In Indiana, it rained at least once a week, and no one commented on it. The temperatures in Shipshe rarely passed the mid-80s. Life was different here, and he'd grown used to it. He liked it, though Becca had teased him more than once about their snowy winters. He thought he wouldn't mind a little snow if it meant he could walk through it with Becca.

He whistled as he harnessed Samson. The gelding even seemed pleased with the weather. Gideon would put in half a day's work, then see if Becca wanted to go for ice cream. He'd missed talking with her the day before. It was rare for a day to pass when they didn't see each other.

Thirty minutes later, he'd handed Samson off to the Amish kid who was working the parking area and hustled over to the loading dock. They were expecting quite a few supplies, and he wanted to be there to check everything off and to be sure items were forwarded to the correct department.

He'd barely made it to the loading area when Samuel thrust a note into his hand. "From the boss..."

The note was in Amos's handwriting and was short and to the point.

See me as soon as you arrive.

Gideon passed his clipboard to Samuel and headed over to the office.

"Shut the door, please."

Yikes. He'd only ever had one closed-door meeting with Amos, and that had been when he'd first arrived. The day he'd met Becca. He almost laughed at that memory. She'd seemed to be everything that irked him in a woman—opinionated, stubborn, blunt. Now those were three of the things that he loved about her.

"Becca asked me to give this to you. If you'd like, I can give you a moment alone."

Gideon reached for the envelope. He heard Amos, but the words didn't register. He was completely focused on ripping open the envelope.

Why would Becca write him a letter?

He read it quickly, then glanced up at Amos to see if this was some sort of joke. Amos's expression was quite serious. No joke, then.

He read it again.

Dear Gideon,
I'm so sorry that I didn't get to say goodbye in
person. MDS called yesterday. They were desper-
ate for volunteers in North Carolina and asked if
I could leave immediately. I'll write as soon as I
arrive.
Yours,
Becca

He stared at the page a moment, but the words written there didn't change. "I don't understand. She's gone?"

"Ya."

"To North Carolina?"

"Ya."

He turned the single sheet of paper over, but there was nothing written on the back. "I knew she was planning on going, maybe in the fall or even in January..."

His words trailed off. He couldn't shake the feeling that this was all a dream—a very bad and confusing dream. Soon, he'd look down to see he'd forgotten to put on his pants and shoes.

But it wasn't a dream.

Becca was really and truly gone.

Amos's chair creaked as he leaned back in it. "She received a call after lunch, came to me and asked my opinion. Maybe she was asking my permission. I'm not really sure. With women, it's sometimes hard to tell exactly what they want to hear."

"And what did you tell her?"

"That I was fine physically, and that you were competently taking care of all her prior responsibilities. I told her that she was free to go."

Gideon didn't answer that. He didn't know how to answer it.

Amos tapped the table, causing Gideon to look up. "I'll tell you what I told her, son. The bus runs both ways. Anytime she's ready to come home, she's welcome. We can trust her to know when that time is. *Ya?*"

"You're right. I'm just surprised, is all."

"Sometimes our mind is ready for a thing, but our heart insists on lagging behind a bit."

His heart was lagging behind, that was for certain. Gideon went through the day in a bit of a fog—and the day after that as well. He kept expecting to see Becca when he walked around a corner in the office or approached a vendor's stall. He listened for her laugh, caught himself looking twice at a woman driving a buggy. But Becca was gone. One way or another, he was going to have to learn to live with that.

He forced himself to focus on his work.

He haunted the mailbox.

He wrote her letters in response to her single-page goodbye, but he didn't send them. He tore them up because he sounded like a lovesick pup.

Finally, on Wednesday of the next week, Nathan met him at the door with a huge smile and an envelope. He placed it gently in Gideon's hands. "Think I'll take myself out to brush Samson."

Gideon wanted to rip open the letter. Instead, he smelled it, then smiled at the familiar handwriting; and finally, he went to the kitchen table, sat down and pulled in a deep breath.

Would this letter break his heart or soothe it?

What did he hope to find in this little envelope? That she was happy and well. That she loved the work. That she missed home and loved him and couldn't stand being away.

That last might be asking a little much for less than a week's separation. He pulled out his pocket knife, slit open the envelope and removed three sheets. Becca's handwriting covered the front and back of each page.

Dear Gideon,

I am so sorry that I didn't speak to you in person before I left. Looking back, I'm not sure why I didn't hire a driver and come up to South Bend. I didn't know what hospital Nathan was in, but certainly there can't be that many hospitals there. Fortunately, as soon as I arrived here in North Carolina, they threw me into work, so I haven't had much time to focus on my regrets.

The bus ride was terrible and wonderful at the same time. It took fifteen hours, so I didn't arrive until nine thirty in the evening. We drove through Ohio, West Virginia, Virginia and then all the way across North Carolina. The community where we're working is only thirty minutes from the coast, though I haven't seen it yet. We're stationed in a small town called Maple Hill.

The hurricane that skirted the East Coast brought heavy rains with it. Many homes in the area were destroyed. Some have mud a foot deep. Mucking out was one of my first assignments. It sounds like what you do with a horse stall, and it is quite similar.

Most of the people I work with are quite experienced at this—two other girls and myself are the only new volunteers. We share a small RV together.

It has a bathroom and tiny kitchen and two bedrooms. Lydia sleeps on the couch. She says that she likes it there, but I suspect she is simply being kind.

Did you know my mamm's name was Lydia? It feels like Gotte's stamp of approval on my being here. That might sound silly. I can see you shaking your head and smiling and telling me to be practical.

From a practical perspective, the work we're doing is quite critical. Most of the homeowners had some form of insurance, but there are no work crews to be had. The waiting lists for a general contractor extend more than four months out. In the meantime, families who have lost their homes live with relatives or stay in hotels if they have the money to do so. Sometimes this means a long commute, as they're still expected to go to their job every day. They are so very grateful for our help.

We've completely cleaned out three homes, which entailed removing everything. We clean what is left with bleach and let it dry. Next week, we begin rebuilding.

I miss my family and the market, and more than anything, I miss you. Still, I do feel as if this is where I'm supposed to be. Please write me and tell me how you are. You can send it to the central MDS address I've included below, and they will forward to our work crew.
Yours,
Becca

Gideon stared at that single word—*yours*. Was she his? Did she love him as he loved her? He thought back to when they'd sat in the field of wildflowers, when he'd told her that he loved her. She'd said that she cared for him too.

He stood and paced the room.

You could care for an old dog, or a job, or an *aenti*. Did she love him as a *fraa* loved a husband? Did she care for him enough to spend the rest of her life with him? Possibly she wasn't sure, or maybe she was simply shy about expressing her feelings.

He'd never known her to be shy about anything.

He'd write her back. He'd do it this very minute.

Then he raised his gaze to the window, remembered that Nathan was out with Samson, realized there were chores to do.

He tucked the sheets of paper back into the envelope and put it on top of the dresser in his room. He'd write her tonight. He'd tell her how proud he was of her, how he missed her, how things weren't the same when she wasn't here.

And he'd tell her that he loved her.

Becca spent three weeks in North Carolina. By mid-September, she was transferred to Tennessee, where fires had ravaged an entire subdivision of homes. She learned to carefully sift through the ashes, setting aside anything that might be of sentimental value to the family. She found a diamond necklace, a tin of old photographs and even an unscathed ceramic statue of Mary and the baby Jesus.

She'd spent only a week in Tennessee when she was reassigned to Alabama. A tropical storm had toppled all the houses along one stretch of beach. These weren't second homes for wealthy tourists; they were the homes of teachers and truck drivers and waitresses. MDS workers, in conjunction with local volunteers, stacked debris on large flatbed trailers, which was driven off to the town's dump. Then they began the process of rebuilding. She was thrilled to be sharing a room with Lydia again. All the workers on the MDS crew had been kind, but she'd felt a special connection with Lydia.

"Still writing your beau every week?"

"Actually, I haven't returned Gideon's letter from earlier this month. Every time I start, the words seem stuck in my throat."

Lydia's eyes widened. "Are you going to break up with him?"

"It's not that. Not really. It's just that it doesn't seem fair to ask him to wait."

"I understand. My *mamm* drops hints in every letter, saying how much I'm missed, how she can't stand the thought of holidays with me wandering around the globe."

Becca laughed and so did Lydia.

"Around the globe, huh?"

"*Ya.* My *mamm* thinks I'm a real globe-trotter."

"I thought I wanted to experience the holidays somewhere different. I even daydreamed about Christmas in the mission field. Now all I can think about is home and how much I miss everyone."

"No doubt that's normal."

"No doubt." But the ache remained, and Becca didn't understand what it meant. She truly loved the work she was doing. At the same time, she was desperate to see her family and Gideon again.

The dinner gong ended their conversation. But as they walked from their little RV to the dining hall, Becca realized that she did like this life. She liked seeing different places, doing different jobs, never knowing what the next day might bring. She'd never seen such tragedy followed by such gratitude. She'd never felt like she was part of something important.

November found her in Florida, helping at an immigrant center. She spent her days washing and handing out donated clothing to families who literally had nothing other than what they were wearing, as well as assisting Samaritan's Purse doctors. Several days a week, she worked in the Red Cross day care, taking care of *kinner* while their parents filled out government paperwork.

Each night, she reread Gideon's letters. There were three now that she'd not answered—each shorter than the last. She still cared for him, but she wasn't ready to go home yet. How could she ask him to wait? Wasn't that expecting too much from someone?

She thought of going home for Thanksgiving, but a freak snowstorm in Massachusetts dumped several feet of snow. It was unusually wet and heavy and caused quite a few roofs to cave in. By this point, she was adept at scrambling up on roofs and helping with tarps. She liked that she wasn't relegated to the kitchen, to women's work—though everyone put in a few shifts a week providing meals and doing cleanup.

She was in the small town of Conway, Vermont, when she felt her first pang of homesickness. Once again rooming with Lydia, they'd been given a rare afternoon off and decided to go to the small downtown shopping area. Every window held a Christmas display. Couples strolled along the sidewalks, hand in hand. Mothers held bundled-up babies.

They'd stopped to eat in a sandwich shop, and even

the music playing softly over the speakers—"God Rest You Merry Gentlemen"—caused her heart to ache.

Lydia's sandwich was halfway to her mouth when she noticed Becca's expression. "What's wrong?"

"I don't know. Nothing. Maybe I'm homesick a little. I guess it's the holidays."

"*Ya.* I've never been away from home at Christmas. Have you?"

"I've never been away from home at all before MDS."

Lydia nodded in understanding and took a large bite of her sandwich. Washing it down with hot chocolate, she reached for a chip and studied Becca.

"What?" Her mind flashed back on the morning she'd shared coffee with Gideon at the Davis Mercantile, when he'd stared at her as if she had her *kapp* on backward, and she'd thought that she had a whipped-cream mustache. Was that when she'd first fallen in love with him? She shook away the thought. "Do I have something on my face?"

"*Nein.* I was just wondering… I don't mean to be intrusive, but could it be that what's bothering you is Gideon?"

Becca stared down at her plate. "I haven't heard from him in some time now."

"Because you stopped writing to him."

"I guess."

Lydia reached across and covered Becca's hands with hers. "Do you care for him?"

"*Ya.* I do." She closed her eyes, then pulled her hands away and scrubbed them across her face. "I suppose I didn't realize just how much until the last week or so."

"Winter is a *gut* time to have a boyfriend—he can

buy you hot chocolate, help you decorate for the holiday, even take you for a buggy ride on a snowy evening."

Becca attempted a laugh. It sounded pitiful even to her ears. She could do all those things herself. She didn't need a beau to buy her hot chocolate or decorate her porch or drive her buggy. But having Gideon beside her as she enjoyed those things—*ya*, that was something she still dreamed of. "I'm not sure Gideon has ever seen more than a dusting of snow."

"So you're missing his first winter up north."

"I am." She nibbled at her sandwich. "Honestly, I'm missing it all—my *schweschdern*, my church, even the market where I worked. Does that sound childish?"

"Not at all."

"Usually we're less busy during the winter, but my *dat* had this wild idea to expand our Christmas market this year. I try to imagine what that looks like, but I come up blank. It's as if I'm slowly forgetting what home looks like."

"You're not forgetting—you're blocking. It's not the same thing."

"I guess. What are you going to do? I know your *mamm* is pressuring you. Will you go home for Christmas?"

"*Ya.* I wrote yesterday and said I'd be home by the middle of December."

"And then? Next year?"

"Who knows." Lydia's eyes sparkled. "I could be married by then."

Lydia left the next week.

Becca felt even more forlorn without her. The new girls she was sharing a trailer with were nice, but they seemed incredibly young and naive. She was almost relieved when the MDS coordinator asked if she'd be willing to head back to Florida.

She stood gaping at the Christmas decorations as soon as she stepped off the bus. It was late in the evening as the MDS coordinator for the area drove her to their lodging. Palm trees stretched twenty feet or more in the air. Tiny white lights had been wrapped around their trunks, with a few feet of red lights near the top and green lights above that to emphasize the swaying palm branches. Giant plastic flamingos adorned people's yards, decked out in festive hats and scarves. It all seemed very foreign and jolly and exactly as she'd dreamed.

Their job site was in the small town of Villa Tasso, which looked out onto the North Channel of the gulf. Houses had been damaged by a hurricane, and they were once again cleaning out mud, bleaching concrete slabs and readying the sites for rebuilding. At night, she'd see Christmas lights stretching down the length of the waterfront area. The days were warm, and the breeze from the gulf was welcome.

Someone on the work crew mentioned that six inches of snow had been dumped on Northern Indiana. They laughed about riding in freezing buggies, having to clear snow and ice off porch steps, bundling up just to walk out to the barn.

But the sunny days and warm temperatures only made her more homesick. She wanted to see her family. She needed to speak with Gideon. She had a lot to explain, even more to apologize for. It was only mid-December, a full ten days until Christmas, but she was ready to go home. Finally resolving that it was time to leave, she walked into the coordinator's office.

"Becca. *Gut* to see you. Have I mentioned how invaluable you arc to our crew? The younger girls all look up to you."

"About that—"

"Uh-oh." Evangeline Brubaker was a fiftysome-thing-year-old widow. She had long hair that reached down her back in a braid and wore the simple Menno-nite handkerchief-style covering. "Sounds as if you have something to tell me."

"I'd like to go home."

"For the holidays?" She consulted her calendar. "We could have you on a bus home on the twenty-third of De-ccmbcr. That would give you time to finish up here—"

"Sooner. If that's possible."

"Oh." Evangeline sat back, pulled off her glasses and cleaned them with the hem of her dress. "Of course, but I'd like to ask what this is about. Is everything all right? Is there any problem with the crew that you'd like to tell me about?"

"No problem at all." Becca sighed. She thought of keeping all her doubts and worries to herself, but Evan-geline was a kind person and a *gut* listener. She needed to talk to someone, and lately she'd found herself hold-ing back even in her letters to her family. She didn't want to worry them. "All my life, I dreamed of leaving our little town."

Evangeline nodded and motioned for her to continue.

"MDS was simply a way to do that. I knew a lit-tle about the work that you did, the people you helped, but not a lot. You know, it was just words on a sheet of paper to me, but that sheet of paper represented my es-cape route."

"People come to serve for different reasons, Becca. The *why* isn't as important as the fact that you are helping people. You're literally being the hands and feet of Christ to those in need."

"I know that now. I understand it in a way I never could have before."

"But—"

"But I still need to go home. I am so sorry."

"There is nothing to apologize for." Evangeline sat up straighter, her hands flat against her desk, her eyes studying Becca. "You've been with us for over four months now. You have been a huge asset to our work crews. As I'm sure you know, many of our volunteers work for a week or two—as their home responsibilities allow."

"Yes, I know that."

"What I'm saying is that you're welcome anytime, for a week, several weeks or an indefinite period. We'll always have a place for you."

"It won't cause any hardship if I go home soon, like this week?"

"It will not. Do what your heart is telling you to do, my dear. Speak to your family, and then let me know what day you'd like to leave. I'll be happy to arrange the transportation, though it will probably be by bus."

Becca almost laughed. She didn't mind riding on the bus, even if it took fifteen hours, even if it took longer. She simply needed to be in Shipshewana for Christmas. She needed to see Sarah and Eunice, Bethany and Ada. She needed to see her father, and more than anything else, she longed to speak to Gideon.

She'd learned many things since leaving Indiana, but chief among them was the fact that plans were good and fine, but they meant nothing if she had to leave all she loved behind her. Why had she ever thought she'd find happiness by running away?

She didn't know if Gideon still loved her or if perhaps he'd changed his mind. Maybe he'd found someone else. But she did know that she needed to see him, she needed to apologize and ask him how he felt. She needed to go home.

Chapter Fourteen

Becca stepped off the bus at six in the evening. Eunice had been waiting for her inside the small station. She'd run outside as soon as Becca had walked down the bus's steps. Now she enfolded her in a hug and laughed.

"We were worried that the snowstorm might have delayed your arrival."

"*Nein.* The roads were *gut.*" Becca was a little surprised that Eunice had been the one to pick her up. As they waited for the bus driver to unload her suitcase, Eunice caught her up on where the rest of the family was.

"Sarah was home, making more baked goods for the market."

"The Christmas thing—I'd forgotten."

"Right. I figured *Dat* had written you about it. Since it's our first year to offer a new and expanded Christmas Market, there's a lot to do. Did Bethany write you that she's running the RV park?"

"We have an RV park?"

"We do now." Eunice laughed again. "Things have changed around here a little."

"I'll say. I've only been gone four months."

"Everyone's glad your home, sis. Christmas wouldn't have been the same with you gone."

Becca didn't trust herself to answer that. Fortunately, the driver found her suitcase and set it next to them. She tipped him a couple of dollars; then she and Eunice hurried across the parking area to the waiting buggy.

The snow crunched under her feet, and she had to pull her coat more tightly around her. The night was cold, and when she looked up, she saw a sky full of stars.

Peanut looked like the same sweet horse that she'd always been. Becca couldn't believe how nice it felt to wrap her arms around the mare. She'd missed everything about their little town, and she'd dreamed of this moment—of coming home—for so many nights that she felt as if she were walking through a dream now.

Eunice hopped up into the buggy but didn't bother turning on the small heater. "Figured you'd want to go by the market and see everyone."

"*Ya.* I'd love to." She was so tired, she could have slept in the buggy, but she also knew she wouldn't rest knowing everyone else was at the market. "Tell me about this RV park and Bethany."

"Oh, well, it's fairly small now, with it being winter and all. Both *Dat* and Gideon figure it will expand in the spring. It started when some vendors came to Gideon and asked if they could park in the back pasture. Then a few of the guests learned about it and wanted to stay as well."

Becca's stomach tightened at the mention of Gideon. Would she see him tonight? Why had she quit writing him? And what should she say to him? How could she possibly explain all that had happened, all she'd seen or how much she'd missed home—missed *him*?

She cleared her throat and tried to focus on what Eunice was saying. "Isn't it awfully cold to be camping in an RV?"

"The full-timers all have generators." They'd pulled out of the parking area and were headed toward the market. The Christmas displays in the stores they passed were brightly lit—the windows filled with evergreen trees, under which were placed quilts and pillows, toys and tins of baked goods. It was a far cry from decorated flamingos, and it looked *wunderbaar* to her eyes.

"And Bethany? She's actually working at this RV park?"

"Sure and certain, she is, and she's *gut* at it. I guess she's a real nester, which is why she enjoyed the crafting so much. It never made her much money, though, and *Dat* needed a manager for the RV park." Eunice shrugged. "You know how persuasive he can be."

"Yes, I do. Is he feeling as well as his letters claimed?"

"Definitely. And Sarah makes sure he goes to all his appointments. His tests came back a few days ago. When that happens, we have a family meeting and go over them. The results were *gut*."

"And you?"

"Still tinkering." Eunice laughed again. She certainly seemed in a fine mood. Her cheeks were rosy, and her eyes sparkled. "Sarah occasionally loses her patience with the dirt and grease I drag inside, but together we're able to do most that needs to be done around the farm."

"And what about Ada? Is she still working as an assistant at the schoolhouse?"

"She is, but she says it's not for her. She claims if she works there much longer, she'll never marry because she won't want children. She's angling to quit the job and find something else, but *Dat* won't hear of it. He said she made a commitment and she's sticking to it through the school year."

"Oh, my."

"Exactly."

Bethany directed Peanut into the parking area, and Becca's mouth gaped. She wasn't sure what she'd envisioned, but it wasn't this. She'd expected a dozen cars and buggies combined, but she was staring out the window at a half-full parking lot. There were a lot of cars and an equally large amount of buggies.

"I can't believe this many people came out on a cold December night."

"Oh, it's the talk of the town—of the entire area, actually. We were even featured in the South Bend paper. Seems folks have been wanting more things to do in the winter, and A Plain & Simple Christmas is just the thing."

Those words—*A Plain & Simple Christmas*—were displayed everywhere Becca looked. On a banner next to the parking booth. On directional signs toward the market area. Even on T-shirts that people were wearing.

Eunice parked the buggy and set the brake as Becca hopped out, patted Peanut and looped his reins around the parking post. She wrapped her scarf more tightly around her neck to keep out the Indiana cold. Hard to believe that twenty-four hours ago, she'd been in Florida where the daytime highs hovered in the low eighties.

The market was exactly as she remembered it while looking quite different at the same time. She again had the disorienting feeling of walking through one of her dreams. The vendor area was empty. The area where the stalls would have been was covered with a fresh coat of snow. Twinkly lights and signs ran alongside the shoveled sidewalk and led them toward the auction area.

When Becca turned the corner and walked into the Plain & Simple Christmas Market, what she saw quite literally took her breath away. The walls of the auction house provided a windbreak. Gas heaters like she'd seen outside *Englisch* restaurants in Massachusetts helped warm the place up enough that people were loosening their scarves and coats. Everywhere she looked, folks were pausing to shop, greet friends, enjoy hot apple cider and hot chocolate. The sounds and smells of the market flooded her senses, and for a moment, she fell into the memories that had formed the person she now was.

A child holding her *dat*'s hand as they walked across a snow-covered field.

A young girl twirling in her new dress that her *mamm* had made.

A gawky teenager, huddling with friends.

A young woman wondering if she'd ever find love.

She was all those things, and yet they were all the old Becca, the one she'd outgrown since leaving home. Her travels had changed her in some way. One thing was certain—they'd made home all the more precious.

Eunice had run off to help someone, and Becca wandered along the aisles until she found herself standing in front of the Christmas crèche.

Had it been last August that her *dat* had first mentioned the idea to her?

The tableau was situated in the far northwest corner. A temporary wall had been positioned behind it to keep the wind at bay. She recognized every single person on that stage—the wise men, the shepherds, Mary, Joseph and even the baby. All were dressed in plain clothes. A goat bleated from where it was bedded down next to a lamb. There was even a donkey to the side, waiting patiently and swishing its tail back and forth.

Becca stood there, immersed in the sights and smells and feel of home, when butterflies swarmed in her stomach and the hairs on her arms stood on end. Then she heard his voice, and her heart seemed to stop beating.

"Becca?"

She turned slowly, knowing who she would see. Every fiber of her being had realized he was near a fraction of a second before he'd spoken. "Gideon. Hi."

"Hi." He stared at her, mouth slightly open, a miniature bale of hay in one hand and a shepherd's staff in the other. "I… I didn't know you were back."

"Just arrived. Eunice brought me straight here from the bus station." She wanted to drink in the sight of him, but she tore her gaze away. She had a dozen questions, and she was afraid to ask a single one. So instead, she said, "This looks *gut*. Very Christmassy and very busy."

"Oh. *Ya*. I guess so. Listen, I have to get this hay over to the petting zoo, and one of our shepherds needs his staff—but don't leave. Okay? Don't…don't go anywhere."

"I won't." She tried to smile, but she was trembling so much that she was afraid it looked like a grimace.

Gideon stepped closer. "I'll be right back."

So she waited, hoping and afraid at the same time. She waited to find out just exactly what she'd come home to.

Gideon was jogging back from the makeshift petting zoo when he passed Amos. He stopped and walked back to the man who was both his boss and his friend. "I saw Becca."

"She looks *gut, ya*? It's *wunderbaar* to have her home."

"Why didn't you tell me?"

Amos reached out and patted his shoulder. "Consider it a Christmas surprise."

But was it a *gut* surprise or a bad one? A perfectly wrapped gift or coal in his *Englisch* stocking? He hurried back to where he'd left her, worried that she would have walked off, disappeared, been a figment of his imagination.

Becca had only moved a few steps closer to the Christmas tableau. She was showing a little *Englisch* girl how to gently pet the donkey so as not to startle it. Gideon stopped and studied her, this woman who had claimed his heart—kneeling beside the girl, a green-and-gray scarf wrapped around her neck, her coat partially open and revealing a navy blue dress. He thought that she was the most beautiful thing he'd ever seen.

He wanted to take her to the buggy, to take her for a ride to somewhere that they could be alone and talk privately.

But there was a Plain & Simple Christmas Market to run.

He'd just stepped forward to touch her arm when James Lapp ran up, breathless and grinning. "The camel sort of got away from Samuel. We're trying to corner it in the parking lot."

"A camel?" Becca stood and cocked her head.

Even that old familiar gesture brought a stab of pain to Gideon's heart, as well as a flutter of joy.

"Oh, hey, Becca. I didn't see you there."

"Hi, James."

"We need your help, Gideon."

At the same moment, Becca's friend, Claire, skidded to a stop in front of them.

"Becca, I didn't know you were back!"

The girls hugged, and then Claire turned to Gideon. "We're completely out of popcorn, and there's a line of folks waiting. Are there more packages of kernels somewhere?"

"*Ya*, in the auction office, but I have to go and help with…"

"The camel. I'll help Claire locate the supplies." Becca smiled, and that smile caused one of the knots in Gideon's stomach to melt away. She headed off toward the auction office, and he jogged toward the parking area.

The next few hours passed in a blur. He'd occasionally catch a glimpse of Becca helping a vendor, passing out hot chocolate, even working at the gift-wrapping table.

Finally, shoppers traipsed back to their cars and buggies, and the place grew blessedly quiet. The market had closed at eight o'clock on the dot, and afterward, the employees all gathered in the diner for a meeting.

"We had a *gut* first day," Amos declared. "We couldn't have done it without each of you. Gideon has a few adjustments to tomorrow's assignments, and then I want everyone to go home and get some rest. We'll see you back here tomorrow afternoon at four o'clock sharp."

Gideon somehow managed to get through the half dozen announcements he had, but his eyes kept straying toward Becca, who was sitting at the back, surrounded by her family.

Becca was home.

Finally.

The question was whether she was here to stay.

He was afraid she might ride home with her family, but she held back and waited for him.

"Can I take you home?"

"I was hoping you might."

How was it that she looked as fresh as a Christmas poinsettia? Hadn't she been traveling all day? Had her last assignment been Florida or Massachusetts? Either way, it was a long bus ride. She didn't look nearly as exhausted as he felt. Gideon thought he could go to bed and sleep a solid twelve hours, but that wasn't quite right. He'd toss and turn and be miserable until he had a few answers—answers that might break his heart or fulfill his dearest dream.

Best to know which as soon as possible.

They walked to the parking area, where the only buggy left was his.

"Is Nathan doing okay?"

"*Ya. Gut.* He wanted to come tonight, but I told him tomorrow would be better. The carolers will be singing."

"You've done a great job, Gideon. When my *dat* told me he wanted to have an expanded Christmas market, I thought he was overreaching. Plainly, I was wrong. Everywhere I looked tonight, guests were having a *wunderbaar* time."

"It's *gut* for our vendors too. They can use the added income this time of year."

He held the buggy door open for her, and when she climbed up into the seat, they were so close that he nearly reached out and pulled her into his arms. He couldn't, though—not until they'd had a chance to talk. If her feelings had changed, he didn't want to make her feel awkward or embarrassed. He didn't want to mess this up now that she was within his reach.

As he drove toward the Yoder farm, snow began falling. He felt as if he was living inside a snow globe. He felt as if he were walking through a dream.

"I've missed this." Becca sighed and hugged her arms around herself. "I never would have guessed how homesick a person could be."

"Tell me about your work."

She seemed to hesitate, then cleared her throat and angled in the seat so that she was facing him. It was all he could do to keep his eyes on the road, though it wouldn't have mattered if he'd dropped the reins altogether. Samson seemed to know where they were going.

"Working with MDS was hard and exciting and more fulfilling than I can describe. The people we helped were so grateful. We'd arrive in an area and see these houses that had been destroyed by floods or fire. We'd meet people who had nothing left, and they would literally weep as we began to rebuild their homes." She stared down at her lap, then glanced back up at him. "It certainly made me appreciate all that we have and the way our community supports one another."

"It sounds amazing."

"*Ya*. It is that."

"And you actually got your hands dirty, huh?"

Becca laughed. "We rotate assignments—so I might be in the kitchen a few days, but then I'd be mucking out houses or nailing in hurricane joists."

Silence enveloped them as Samson trotted the last half mile, and then Gideon directed the gelding down the lane to Becca's home.

Becca's home.

But was it? Or was she leaving again?

He pulled to a stop in front of the house, set the brake

and turned to her. "I know you must be tired, and I won't keep you. But…"

"It's okay, Gideon. You deserve answers."

"Why did you quit writing?"

"Okay. Wow. Straight to the point…" Becca's voice trailed off as she gazed out the buggy window.

"Was it because your feelings changed?"

"Nein." Now she faced him directly. "It's because I was a coward. Okay? I was afraid. I was afraid that you would wait for me, and then I would disappoint you. I didn't… I couldn't bear the thought of you putting your life on hold for me."

"But that wasn't your decision to make."

"Right. You're right." She didn't look away as she asked, "Have *your* feelings changed?"

"No. My feelings for you aren't changeable, Becca. They're as permanent and dependable as snow in Indiana or carols at Christmas or…" But he never finished all the silly analogies that had built up in his mind, because at that moment, Becca threw herself into his arms.

He held her, breathed in the scent of her and had just lowered his lips to hers when the front door of the farmhouse was thrown open. Onto the porch and down the steps tumbled Ada, Sarah, Eunice, Bethany and even Amos. Laughing and hugging and talking, they pulled her from the buggy, up the porch steps and into the house.

Gideon was left standing by the buggy, longing to follow that group into the house and knowing that he needed to give them their private time. The right thing to do was to drive back to Nathan's.

Amos retraced his steps back to the buggy where Gideon stood. Gideon realized that indecision and longing must be etched all over his face. He tried to plaster on a smile.

"It's *gut* to have her home." Amos crossed his arms, rested his backside against the buggy and studied the house.

Gideon could make out the five *schweschdern* in the living room, shadows thrown about by the lamplight. Their merry sounds trickled out to where he waited.

"You're welcome to come in."

"I should go home."

Amos raised an eyebrow, but he didn't try to talk him out of it. They'd grown close since Becca had left—a father who missed his *doschder* and a man who longed for the woman he loved to return.

Now she was home.

And Gideon almost had the courage to believe it meant she was there to stay.

Chapter Fifteen

Gideon was surprised that the next week passed in a blur of activities. He barely had time to worry about his future and hopes and dreams. The final days of the Christmas market were Thursday and Friday. They could have had a huge crowd on Saturday—Christmas Eve—but both Gideon and Amos had carefully planned out the holiday calendar. Christmas Eve was for family and spiritual reflection. It wasn't for profit.

Becca helped at the market every day. She didn't exactly slip into her old role—Gideon had filled that quite adequately—but she had a knack for understanding where help was needed. Before he could even ask, she was there, helping a vendor, finding additional supplies, rounding up sheep.

He'd catch glimpses of her, and each time, it made his heart do a funny thing. It reminded him of the time they'd sat beneath the maple tree when he'd held her in his arms. When he'd told her that he loved her.

He woke Saturday, had breakfast with Nathan and then tended to the outside chores. They'd been invited to share the Christmas meal with Becca's family, and he was looking forward to it. But he needed to see her alone first. He needed to tell her how he felt.

Nathan was fired up for the holiday. He was in full cooking mode and worried when he found that he was missing several ingredients from his Christmas dishes. Gideon made a quick trip to the grocery store, amazed at the crowds standing in line at the bakery, the deli, and of course the checkouts.

Most people raised a hand in greeting or called out to him.

He'd made friends since he moved here.

More importantly, he felt that he was part of the community. Partly, that was because he'd thrown himself into helping anywhere and everywhere after Becca had left. He'd calmed his own worries by staying busy. Now he felt as if the people around him were part of his extended family. Honestly, he couldn't imagine living anywhere else.

His years in Beeville, Texas, seemed like a different life.

He'd enjoyed his visit back home in September, but being there had only served to remind him that his home was here now.

He'd mailed his Christmas letter and some small gifts to his parents the week before. On the off chance that he might catch someone, he stopped by the phone shack on his way back to Nathan's. He was surprised when his *dat* answered.

They spoke of work, the holidays, how his siblings were doing and his *mamm*. Finally, his *dat* asked, "Did she come back?"

"*Ya.* She did."

"And are you going to ask her?"

"I am."

There was silence for a moment, and Gideon had the fleeting worry that his *dat* was unhappy with that decision. Then he heard him drop the receiver, fumble around for something and blow his nose. He'd only ever seen his *dat* tear up a few times in his life. Had his father been that worried about him?

"That's *gut*, son. We'll be praying for you both."

"Danki."

"You write us as soon as you have her answer."

"I will."

"And, Gideon…"

There was a pause that seemed to carry the weight of their history, the disagreements and hard feelings, the unwelcome advice, the phone calls and letters and prayers.

"We're proud of you, and we love you."

Why was it that those simple words meant so much to him? He wasn't the uncertain young man who had arrived in Indiana eight months earlier. He was more confident—more prayerful, if he was being honest. Still, having his father's blessing seemed like the perfect Christmas gift.

He took the missing ingredients back to Nathan, then said, "I have an errand to run. I'll be back in time for dinner."

Nathan's eyes twinkled as he turned back toward the stove. "Tell Becca hello for me."

The guy was eighty-seven—soon to be eighty-eight—and still he didn't miss a thing.

Gideon's nerves returned as he headed toward Becca's. What if he flubbed this up? Would it be better to wait? What if she said no?

He wasn't going to flub it up. He was going to be honest.

He was done keeping his feelings and hopes and dreams to himself. It was time to tell Becca all that was in his heart.

If she said no, then he'd deal with that somehow.

The sun was angling toward the horizon as he pulled into the Yoder farm. Another inch of snow had fallen during the night. Everything looked pristine and festive.

He walked up the steps of the porch and nearly collided with Ada, who'd come around the corner of the porch.

"Gideon! Perfect timing. You can open the door for me." Her arms were full of pine cones and sprigs of holly. She popped through the door ahead of him and moved back toward the bedrooms, singing, "We bake you a merry Christmas..."

The living room was decorated with more pine cones and holly. Someone had even strung popcorn and placed it across the fireplace mantel. And the smells coming from the kitchen could rival that of Nathan's cooking. From the sounds of things, the rest of the family was gathered in there.

He stopped in the doorway, completely unsurprised by what he saw. Bethany sat at the table, embroidering what looked like a pillowcase. Sarah stood at the stove, stirring something in a pot. Eunice was attempting to wrap what looked like a tiny birdbath. And Becca?

Becca was frosting a cake. When she glanced up and saw him, her eyes widened, and a smile spread across her face.

"Gideon. What a nice surprise."

"I was wondering if you'd have time for a short walk.

The snow has stopped and it's..." His voice faltered, and his mind went blank. Then he glanced toward the window. "It's beautiful outside."

"Oh. I'd love to, but I'm helping Sarah get all the food together for tonight and..."

Sarah reached over and took the knife Becca had been using to spread the frosting. "We've got this. You've been in here all day. Go."

"Yes, go," repeated Bethany. "You've done nothing but work since you've been home."

"Those MDS people certainly upped your work ethic." Eunice ducked when Becca threw an oven mitt at her.

"I guess I'm going for a walk."

The snow made a nice crunchy sound as they walked toward the barn. They walked shoulder to shoulder, as they used to at the market—as he hoped they always would.

Skirting the barn, they headed toward the pond. Amos had set up a picnic table there in the fall. It was under the shade of two trees, and Gideon had dreamed of proposing to her there. Now his dream was coming true.

Then Becca bent down, gathered up a handful of snow and tossed it at him. He brushed the snow off his coat. "Seriously?" She was gathering more snow and laughing. When he reached down to pack together his own snowball, she hit him with another.

"Oh, you're going to get it now."

"Really? You think you can catch me?"

She took off, laughing and glancing back over her shoulder, occasionally pausing to gather another handful of snow. He almost caught her twice, but she was quicker than he would have guessed. By the time she collapsed by the pond—not at the picnic table but on the opposite side in the open—they were both out of breath.

It wasn't the way he'd dreamed of it.

Nope. This was even better.

"Marry me."

"What?" She'd been lying back, making a snow angel. Now she sat up and stared at him as if she couldn't believe her ears—as if she was surprised.

"Let's get married. Be my *fraa* and have my children, grow old with me, spend a lifetime with me. Say yes, Becca. I love you."

She traced a pattern in the snow.

He inched closer, worry rising in his heart because she hadn't answered. He waited—hoping and praying and wondering what she was thinking as she stared down at the snow between them.

And then he looked down and saw that she'd actually written a word.

Yes.

Becca had written her answer in the snow. She was afraid her voice would betray her, that she'd dissolve into a river of tears and never be able to voice her answer to this very important question that Gideon had asked.

So she'd written those three letters in the snow and waited.

Gideon stared at her, then stared at the note in the snow. When he finally understood that was her answer, he let out a whoop that her family had probably been able to hear in the house. He pulled her to her feet, spun her around and then wrapped his arms around her.

And then he kissed her.

When she was finally able to catch her breath, she reached up and touched his face. "You seem surprised."

"*Nein.* I mean—not really. I'd hoped, but I didn't want to presume."

"I love you, Gideon. I've loved you for a long time."

"Really?"

"The day we were sitting in the field of wildflowers. I knew then."

"You didn't tell me."

"I know, and that was a mistake."

"If you knew you loved me, why did you leave?"

She shrugged and reached for his hand. They slowly began walking back toward the house. It wasn't quite dark yet, but she could see the Christmas candles glowing in the windows.

"Maybe I didn't tell you because my feelings scared me. I guess I was worried that if I admitted I loved you, then I'd never go. Going had become so important to me. It had become a thing all its own. You know?"

He nodded, but he still looked puzzled.

"I loved seeing new places, and I loved the work we did. But those things aren't enough if it means leaving the people I care about the most."

They retraced their steps around the barn, then stopped under the roof's eave, standing shoulder to shoulder with her hand clasped in his. She stared down at that—their two hands—and marveled that it could make her world feel so very right.

"I want to be here with you, even if it means I never travel again."

"Maybe we can find a way to do both."

"*Ya?*" She cocked her head and studied him. "Tell me more."

"Christmas is tomorrow."

"Indeed."

"We could marry by spring."

"That would be quick, but my *dat* would probably agree."

"The market doesn't open until May."

"True."

"How about we combine our honeymoon with a MDS mission?"

The words were barely out of his mouth when she threw herself into his arms.

"I'll take that as a yes."

"*Ya.* That's a yes."

They kissed again, then walked the final few steps toward the house.

"I can't believe we had a snowball fight. You never struck me as a snowball-fight kind of girl."

"Oh, really?"

"Yes."

Her dream of traveling had become such a burden that she'd forgotten how to enjoy life. She'd forgotten that here and now was just as important as tomorrow. Since she'd been home, she'd felt like herself again—she'd felt unencumbered and free and happy. She didn't explain all of that as they tromped up the steps of the porch. Instead, she sent him a sassy smile. "I guess there's still a lot about me for you to learn."

They walked into the house.

Ada was setting the table, singing, "Rolling through the snow." Bethany had folded up her handiwork and was stowing it in her project bag. Eunice stood at the sink, washing grease off her hands. And Sarah was pulling fresh bread from the oven.

Her *dat* was already seated at the table. He looked up at them and smiled. Then he said, "Let's all sit down. I believe Becca and Gideon have some news to share."

* * * * *

If you loved this story,
pick up the other books in the
Indiana Amish Brides series
from bestselling author Vannetta Chapman

A Widow's Hope
Amish Christmas Memories
A Perfect Amish Match
The Amish Christmas Matchmaker
An Unlikely Amish Match
The Amish Christmas Secret
The Baby Next Door
An Amish Baby for Christmas
The Amish Twins Next Door

Available now from Love Inspired!

Find more great reads at www.LoveInspired.com

Dear Reader,

Have you ever had a goal that took on a life of its own? Something that you longed for, dreamed about, and planned for? Sometimes when we reach those goals, they live up to our expectations—and sometimes they don't.

Becca has a goal to see the world, or at least more of the United States. She loves her family, her home, and even her job...but her heart yearns for something different. Gideon, on the other hand, wants what is familiar. He's not a fan of change, and he doesn't see any need to do something or be somewhere different.

And yet sometimes when we plan, God smiles. Sometimes our plans are not what He has in mind for us. The challenge for Becca and Gideon is whether they're willing to put aside these long-held dreams and embrace a future full of promise.

I hope you enjoyed reading *An Amish Proposal for Christmas*. I welcome comments and letters at vannettachapman@gmail.com.

May we continue "giving thanks always for all things unto God the Father in the name of our Lord Jesus Christ" (Ephesians 5:20).

Blessings,
Vannetta

Get 4 FREE REWARDS!

We'll send you 2 FREE Books plus 2 FREE Mystery Gifts.

FREE Value Over **$20**

Both the **Love Inspired®** and **Love Inspired®** **Suspense** series feature compelling novels filled with inspirational romance, faith, forgiveness, and hope.

HARLEQUIN
PLUS

Announcing a **BRAND-NEW** multimedia subscription service for romance fans like you!

Read, Watch and Play.

Experience the easiest way to get the romance content you crave.

Start your **FREE 7 DAY TRIAL** at www.harlequinplus.com/freetrial.